Lock Down Publications and Ca$h Presents

KILLA CREW 2

HONOR THY JACKBOY

Written By
ARYANNA

First Edition 2025

Printed in the United States of America

This is a work of fiction. Names, characters, places, and incidents either are products of the author's imagination or are used fictitiously. Any similarity to actual events or locales or persons, living or dead, is entirely coincidental.

Lock Down Publications
P.O. Box 944
Stockbridge, GA 30281
www.lockdownpublications.com

Like our page on Facebook: Lock Down Publications
www.facebook.com/lockdownpublications.ldp

Stay Connected with Us!

Text **LOCKDOWN** to 22828 to stay up-to-date with new releases, sneak peaks, contests and more…

Like our page on Facebook:
Lock Down Publications

Join Lock Down Publications/The New Era Reading Group

Visit our website:
www.lockdownpublications.com

Follow us on Instagram:
Lock Down Publications

Email Us: We want to hear from you!

Dedication

This book is dedicated to the DMV for making me and loving me.

Acknowledgements

All glory to God because without him I can accomplish nothing. I remain humble in the huge shadow u cast. I wanna thank my fans for allowing me to still be apart of ur lives after a decade of pushing this pen. I DON'T GET TIRED! In that same vein, I gotta thank Cash and LDP for weathering the storms that have changed the game and industry so much in the last 10 years. The longevity we have speaks to the leadership we follow. Special shout out to Queen Coffee watching over us because ur in every line that any of us pens. I wanna thank my family for the good and bad because its all a lesson either way. Shout out to my peoples behind the g-wall holding shit down. I pray we all know freedom one day, and let it be sooner than later because DAMN I'm sick of this shit!!!! I spend a lot of days reflecting on self, seeing the path taken and understanding why it couldn't have happened any other way. I suggest u do the same. To my kids, I pray that peace is what u seek because it far outweighs the immediate gratification that comes from warfare. U don't have blood on ur hands or ur conscience, so keep it that way. On a side note, I've been in a lot of relationships since I've begun this journey of writing, and I've wasted a lot of ink on people I thought would withstand the test of time. So many didn't make it, and I don't say that bitterly, I say it with joy. Fuck love, give me loyalty! FACT$$$

Chapter 1

Kwan

The look of utter anguish on my wife's face didn't bring me any type of joy, but I knew that I had to put my emotions aside and stand on bidness.

"20 seconds to choose who lives and who dies," I said, not looking at my watch because my eyes were glued to Kyndra's.

When she picked the pistol up that I'd slid her way, I saw the light of determination burning brightly through the tears clouding her vision, and I knew in that moment she'd made her decision. Given the fact that the blame for all of the bullshit could be placed squarely on her father's shoulders, I expected her to level the gun at him and pull the trigger. Instead, she did the unthinkable, and before I realized it I'd jumped to my feet.

"What are you doing?" I asked, feeling panic along my nerve endings.

"You told me to choose, and this is my choice. I choose to kill myself because ultimately it was me who gave Skylar the order to silence Rashawna," she replied, calmly cocking the hammer in the pistol that was pressed to her temple.

"Stop, dammit!" I yelled, quickly rounding the table and snatching the loaded gun from her grip.

"Kwan, I really do love you, and I'm more sorry than words can express about having your baby shot and your child killed, but I'm asking that me sacrificing my life be enough."

KILLA CREW 2 | ARYANNA

Part of my brain was screaming that she was bluffing, and self-preservation would stop her from pulling the trigger if I gave her the gun back. The problem was that I was unwilling to call her bluff or gamble with her life. As crazy as it would sound if I verbalized my thoughts, I couldn't see my life without this phenomenal woman beside me. When I looked to Jayson I'd expected to find impatience or anger at my indecision, but instead I saw understanding as his eyes darted to Tink and then came back to mine. I wasn't particularly worried about my brother's judgement of me for actually loving my wife enough to forgive her, however, it did put my mind at ease to know that he was obviously as in love as I was. I tucked my pistol into my pants and pulled Kyndra out of the chair into my arms.

"I can't lose you too, bae," I said, wrapping my arms around her.

"You don't have to...but can you ever forgive me?" She asked softly.

"Time heals all wounds, and I'm willing to give us time," I replied sincerely.

I felt her nod as she laid her head against my chest, and I rested my chin on the top of her head while I stroked her back gently.

"Jayson, do you hate me...or can we take a page out of their book?" Tink asked, slowly rising to her feet and moving to where he was still seated.

"I don't hate you. Truthfully, I love you, and I've never said that to another woman," he replied, opening his arms to her.

The tears that began to stream down her face were obviously those of happiness, but I still saw worry in her eyes.

"I love you too, Jay, but I need to tell you something... I-I think that I'm pregnant."

The way my brother's mouth fell open was comical, causing me to snicker at his shock until I felt Kyndra poke me in my ribs.

"I wouldn't laugh too hard if I were you because I ain't seen my period in a minute," she said, looking up at me with a shy smile.

For a moment I just stared at her, and then I felt my own mouth hit my chest as her words and their potential meaning sank in.

"This is all very touching, but will one of you silly ass females insist that I be untied," Big Hands said, impatiently.

"I'm sorry, did you think that this let you off the hook for the shit you did, bitch nigga?" I asked, looking at him with pure disgust.

"You really think that my daughter is gonna let you kill me, and still love you the same way?" He countered smugly.

"Yeah, that's exactly what I think," I replied, pulling my pistol back out.

"Kwan, wait. There's information we need," Kyndra said, stepping out of my arms and turning her attention to her father.

I didn't say anything, but the gun remained in my palm, ready to knock chunks of this nigga's brain matter out until he was like a pumpkin on Halloween.

"The only info I've got for you is that you better untie me right-the-fuck-now," Big Hands growled angrily.

"First, you need to tell us the whole story behind the gold and platinum bars that you had us jack. We know that the fed Kwan killed was pulling a triple cross with you," Kyndra said.

"A triple cross? Nah, we pulled one of the coldest heists in history, but your dumb ass fucked shit up, and then you let your reckless ass nigga kill a fed. You're trying to get us all killed. So, if you wanna avoid that then I suggest you give me everything that was in those trucks," he stated, sneering at his daughter.

"Giving you that shit ain't gonna change the facts that the fed is dead and the cartel got robbed, so stop trying to spin us," I said, growing more impatient with each word that this nigga spoke.

"Think whatever you wanna think, Kwan, but don't bitch up when niggas come for your head," he replied with a sadistic smile on his face.

"If they come for my husband then they're coming for me. Are you okay with that?" Kyndra asked.

"You made your decision... But if you give me my shit back then I'll protect you," he bargained.

Just hearing him negotiate with his daughter's life over some money, no matter how much money it was, made me wanna shoot this nigga right between the eyes. I raised my gun with the intention of doing just that, but Kyndra put her hand on my arm while looking back at me.

"Baby, he ain't worth the bullet," she said sadly.

I disagreed based on principle and my instincts, but for her sake I restrained myself from pulling the trigger. Instead, I looked at Jayson and gave him a slight nod, which prompted him to get up and smack Kyndra's dad over the head with his own pistol. Big Hands immediately slumped and succumbed to unconsciousness.

"Put him back in the trunk," I demanded.

"I'll grab his feet," Tink offered.

Jayson smiled at her, and they quickly removed the body from the room.

"Can we speak somewhere else?" Kyndra asked, looking up at me.

I started to ask her why, but then I remembered that her dead friend's head was still thawing out on the table like a Thanksgiving Turkey. I nodded while taking her hand in mine, and leading the way back upstairs to our bedroom. Once we got there I started to lead her outside so that we could take in the beautiful sunrise, but she pulled me into the bathroom and immediately turned on the shower.

"You need to take a shower," she said.

I didn't argue with her because I knew that she was undoubtedly struggling with the fact that I'd killed one of her best friends. I wanted to apologize and explain that it was just business, but I knew that she understood that without me offering any hollow platitudes of regret.

I put my gun on the sink and quickly stripped off my bloody clothing, and then I pulled her into my arms. She didn't say a word as I pulled my T-shirt off of her, and then I led her into the shower with me.

Once we were closed in amongst the steam facing each other, there was an awkward tension between us, and I wasn't exactly sure how to fix it. We simply stood there with the hot water pounding our bodies, only inches apart, but feeling like we were separated by millions of miles. The sadness in her eyes gripped my heart and squeezed it until it broke me, and I was forced to make the next move for the both of us.

I'd halfway expected some resistance when I pulled her into my arms, but she came willingly and offered me her mouth when I leaned down towards her. Our kiss was full of its usual passion that only made the shower water around us hotter, and suddenly all coherent thought was fading fast. I lifted her off her feet like she weighed nothing at all, putting her back against the wet wall and then pushing my throbbing dick inside her. The gasp of desire that rolled off of her tongue was swallowed by me, adding to the vibration of the low growl rumbling in my throat. I knew this wasn't a love making type of moment, so I was merciless with the dick and trying to make my presence known in her stomach with every stroke. I fucked her hard and fast until I felt her pussy blossom like the beautiful flower that it was and drench me with her summer rain. I could feel her body trembling with both excitement and the remnants of her first orgasm shifting gears to build towards her second one.

I quickly dropped her to her feet, spun her face first against the wall, and then I drove my dick back inside her with enough force to push her up on the balls of her feet. I used my left hand to brace against the wall, while my right hand wrapped around her delicate neck and applied the pressure that I knew she liked. Her pussy's grip was like a car compactor, fighting me in ways that made it hard for my eyes to stay focused as my knees banged like a drummer kicking a big bass. Still, I didn't slow down. I fucked her harder, but this time when I sensed her flower opening I pollinated it with my cum in hot waves until we were both spent. It was suddenly so hot in the shower that I could barely breathe, but the feeling of satisfaction was undeniable. I pulled out of her and leaned my back against the wall next to her, feeling closer to her, but still very much aware of the distance between us.

"What are you thinking?" I asked softly, looking over at her.

She didn't meet my gaze, and at first she didn't say anything in response. I didn't push, choosing to give her all the patience that she needed.

After a few moments she turned towards me and I could see the tears clouding the beauty of her hazel eyes. "Can you- Can you ever truly forgive me?" She asked.

"Can *you* forgive *me*?"

"Forgive you for what?" She asked, looking confused.

"For Skylar."

The mention of her friend's name caused her to close her eyes for a few seconds, and when she opened them, I could see her pain clearly.

"I can forgive you for that because I feel like it was more my fault than yours. I could've done the job myself, but I sent her to do the dirty work...and I know what that cost you. So how can you ever forgive me or even love me?" She asked.

"Because I know your heart and what your intentions were. No one understands this game and the consequences better than me, and it's that understanding that allows me to forgive you."

I could see that she was absorbing my words, but there was still doubt swimming within the waters of her unshed tears. I pulled her into my arms and kissed her softly before I spoke again.

"Sweetheart, you know that I knew your father before you and I ever met, and I know just how ruthless he can be. I have no doubt that his orders to you would've been nonnegotiable, and we both know the penalty for what he considers to be treason, so I promise you that I understand what happened. And I love you regardless," I said sincerely.

"Are you mad that I didn't let you kill my father?"

"Mad? No, but I think it's a mistake to leave him alive and free to make a move against us," I replied.

"I saw the way that he is around you, and even though I've never seen him scared of a soul in my life, I *know* that he don't want no smoke with you."

"Be that as it may, if he comes at you then he's coming at me, and I've got a feeling that the lick you pulled on that cartel caravan is too much for him to simply let go of," I said.

"Well, I'm damn sure not giving that shit back, so what's our next move?" She asked, looking at me with determination and trust.

I knew the inevitable truth that she was desperately avoiding, and I understood her reasoning, but eventually she was gonna have to face the demon that her father was. I knew that she wasn't ready to do that now, so my focus had to be on how to keep us both alive.

"I think that our best move is to take a long vacation and fall off the radar for a while. Your father doesn't know where we are, so drugging him and dropping him back in Jersey won't be a problem. All we gotta do after that is decide where we wanna go," I said.

"What do we do with everything that we just moved out here?"

"I've got an idea, but you might not like it," I replied, somewhat hesitantly.

She didn't say anything, she simply looked at me expectantly.

"Okay, so we know that the gold and platinum is worth more than the fentanyl, so I say that we keep the bars and use the dope to buy an army," I said.

"An army? What do we need an army for?" She asked, looking confused and skeptical.

"Because we've both made some powerful enemies. By now I'm sure that you've put the pieces together about the robbery at the gallery in L.A when we bumped into each other. I didn't know that we were robbing the Chinese triad, but I do know that they're formidable."

"That was a helluva move you pulled, by the way, but you're right to be worried about the triad. I don't know if they're worse than the cartel, but I'm starting to see why we're gonna need an army. Where do we get one?"

"We'll figure that out once we're settled somewhere else. For now, we need to get your father back stateside, bury the gold and platinum in our backyard here, and stash the dope in a place where whoever we decide to employee can retrieve it with minimal risk."

"Sounds like a lot of work, so I'ma need more motivation," she replied, smiling mischievously.

"What do you have in mind?"

The answer to my question came in the form of her dropping to her knees and taking my dick into her mouth swiftly. After that I found it impossible to concentrate because she was blowing my mind.

Chapter 2

Kyndra

3 months later off the coast of Morocco

"Good morning, baby."

"Kwan, stop. You know that your scruffy beard tickles my stomach when you do that," I said, giggling as he kept kissing my barely visible baby bump.

I never would've imagined that this big, bad killa would be reduced to putty by something as simple as me being pregnant, but he'd definitely become a softy, and I was loving every moment.

"Woman, didn't I tell you about interrupting me when I'm talking to my baby? You'll get your time in a little while," he said, going back to whispering to my stomach.

I didn't even know if our baby could actually hear him, but I prayed that they could so that he or she would always know how much they were loved. Neither of us would be the conventional parent, but we agreed that giving our baby all the love in the world was the most important thing.

"Your mommy be trying to monopolize my time, but don't you worry because I'ma always make sure that you come first, little one."

"That sounds good, but that'll have to wait until he or she gets here because right now your job is to make sure mommy is happy," I said, placing my hands on his head and pushing it lower as I opened my thick thighs.

"Mmm, you're lucky that I'm hungry," he murmured.

I started to say something smart, but his lips were already wrapped around my clit and that shit felt too good. My fingers became entangled in his dreadlocks, but I wasn't pulling on them, I was using them to stay anchored to the bed. The gentle rocking of the 60-foot luxury yacht that we'd made our home since leaving Greece was giving me that feeling of lazy love making on a water bed, and it was hypnotizing.

"Eat this pussy, baby," I whispered, putting my legs on his shoulders.

He obliged me by using his skillful tongue to dive in between my pussy lips in a dance so graceful that it would remind one of an Avatar who knew the ways of water. I struggled valiantly to keep my spine intact, but as soon as he hit my g-spot with his fingers, I bent to his will and my back arched up off the bed. I felt positively possessed, and I *loved* it! Within a few minutes I was cumming so hard that I was worried that I might drown my nigga, but he drank me down like an ice-cold beer on a hot summer day. By the time he climbed from in between my still trembling thighs I was fighting the heaviness of my eyelids, and the nap that was calling me.

"Oh, so you think you're gonna get your nut and just pass out on me?" He asked, laughing.

"Baby, you know that your head game is that pressure, so it's your fault that sleep is the number two side effect."

"What's the number one side effect?"

"Satisfaction," I replied, stretching like a big tabby cat who'd just finished licking herself clean.

He laughed again while pulling me into his arms so that I could lay my head on his chest. I ran my fingers up and down his tight abs, secretly admiring the work that he'd been putting in by using the gym on the yacht. Both he and Jayson had gotten shredded, much to mine and Tink's delight, and now Kwan was 6'4", 280 pounds of solid muscle. In his arms my 5'0", 140 pounds felt tiny and I loved that, especially because I knew that I was gonna get bigger. I knew that Tink probably felt the same as me because Jayson was only an inch shorter than Kwan and a little lighter, but Tink was an inch shorter than me. She was four months pregnant compared to my three and half months, and had already gained 10 pounds that she claimed made her feel huge except for when she was with her nigga. She was barely 115 pounds, so I knew that she was being dramatic, but I loved her enough not to say that to her face.

"Are you hungry, sweetheart?" He asked.

"You already know the answer to that question."

He laughed, but like the great husband that he was he got up out of the bed and left our cabin to go get me some food. I was absolutely spoiled rotten, and I didn't try to deny it because it felt amazing.

I was laying there thinking about calling Tink, when my phone suddenly started vibrating on the nightstand next to the bed. "This bitch must have telepathy," I said aloud, reaching for the phone. I expected to see Tink's face on my screen, but instead I got a surprise that made my heart beat faster. "Hey, Skii, what's up?" I asked, answering her call.

"Is everything good? Don't lie to me either, Kyndra, because I'm not a kid."

Admittedly Skii was 23 years old, and she took care of herself, but at the end of the day she was still Skylar's younger sister, and it was my job to look after her. Especially because I felt like I'd gotten her sister killed.

"Why are you asking me if I'm good when you know that I'm on vacation being pampered?" I countered.

"Because your pops is looking for you, and if he don't know where you are then shit must not be good. So, what's up?"

"Wait, how do you know that my father is looking for me?" I asked, feeling a touch of panic.

"Come in, Kyn, you know that I've kept my ear to the street trying to find a lead on my sister's killer. Not to mention that I was trained by the best hacker that either of us knew."

I couldn't deny the truth in her last statement because Skylar had definitely given Skii the game, and based on what I'd seen I would make the argument that the student was better than her teacher. That didn't cause any feelings of panic when it came to the possibility of her efforts leading back to my doorstep because I knew that Kwan had covered his tracks well enough. To the world, Skylar had simply vanished, but Skii's gut had told her that her big sister was indeed dead, and I'd agreed to that theory simply to spare Skii the crushing blow of false hope. Selfishly, that was all the hope I'd been able to give her, but the fact that I was running for my life sold the idea that I was trying to avoid Skylar's fate. The only thing that threatened my web of lies was my father's persistence in trying to find me.

"Tell me exactly what you heard," I said, sitting up in bed and swinging my feet to the floor.

"I didn't hear a lot, but its weird because he's making inquiries into your whereabouts like you're an opp instead of his daughter. My sister told me before how ruthless and unreasonable your dad can be, but there's no way he'd actually be *after you*...right?"

For a moment I was unsure of how to answer that question, even though I secretly knew the truth. Kwan warned me that this could happen, but my heart had refused to accept the truth that my own father could love money more than me. Despite how many times he'd had me risk my life for the spoils that he'd received.

"I doubt that he's after me; he's probably just looking for me because he's ready to put us back to work. I'm not ready for that," I replied, telling part of the truth and more of a lie.

"I get that. You know that you don't have to do any of it by yourself though. You and Tink are like sisters to me too, and when it comes time for you to fill Skylar's spot on your

17

team, you better know that it won't be by anyone except for me."

"I know, Skii. I love you and I'll call you in a few days. Let me know if you hear anything else."

"I gotchu, and I love you, too," she replied, disconnecting the call.

I don't know how long I sat there with my phone in my hand, just thinking, but I felt Kwan's presence when he came back into the room and I looked up.

"What's wrong?" He asked, stopping in his tracks.

"You're not gonna like it."

"That don't matter because it don't change the fact that something is wrong. Now, what is it?" He asked, crossing to me and sitting the tray of food on the bed beside me.

When I looked up at him all I saw was love in his eyes, and that helped to calm me down.

"I got a call from Skii, Skylar's little sister, and she said that my father is looking for me."

"How reliable is her info?" He asked calmly.

"Well, she's as good a hacker, if not better, than her sister was and she's got her ears to the street."

I watched as Kwan processed this information, while turning his gaze out the window to the calm water surrounding us. I knew that he wasn't particularly worried about anyone running down on us in our current location, especially since we'd built a literal army of Somali pirates to protect us on the water. I had a feeling in the pit of my stomach that I knew what my husband was thinking, even though the words hadn't been spoken aloud in months. When he finally looked back at me I saw the inevitable truth in the thundering storm clouds moving within his eyes.

"What do you wanna do?" He asked.

The question sounded innocent enough, but I'd come to know this man almost as well as I did myself. I would've bet my ovaries that somewhere in his mind laid a flawless battle ready approach that would surely end my father's days on this earth, but he wouldn't execute that plan without my approval. Part me loved him for respecting me that much, but the other part of me wished he'd just take control and do what I was unwilling to do.

"I don't know what I want anymore, Kwan. I mean at this point it feels like we've got more enemies at our throat than friends who could sit around our dinner table with us. How do we bring our child into that type of world?"

"Bae, I promise that I won't let anything happen to you or our child," he said, squatting down in front of me and taking my hands in his.

"I love you, and I know your heart means those words, but there's no way that you can keep that promise," I replied softly, fighting against the tears clogging my throat.

"I *can* keep that promise because I'll murder any and everyone who could possibly present a threat. All you have to do is say the word."

The fire in his eyes blazed like volcanic lava was its power source, and that shit was as intimidating as it was sexy. I'd never known a nigga like Kwan, let alone been loved by one, but I knew that I was as safe as I could possibly be with him.

"I can't-I can't tell you to kill my dad, bae, even though I know that it would make shit easier on all of us," I said.

"Okay, so what if I didn't kill him? What if I simply made his world smaller and neutralized him?"

"How would you do that?" I asked, curious and slightly apprehensive.

"I've got some ideas, but in your condition, I don't wanna stress you out with the details. I just need you to trust me," he said, kissing the backs of my hands.

I felt no hesitation within me when it came to giving this man all my trust to match all my love, but I didn't like the fact that he was getting ready to put me on the sideline. I felt like we were ultimately stronger together, and I'd feel more than a little guilty if anything happened to him without me there to watch his back. Given everything that had happened, and what we'd both lost, I knew that there was no way he'd let me put myself and our baby in danger. That left me little option except to do shit his way.

"I trust you, Kwan, but I swear to God that if you get yourself killed, I'll never forgive you for leaving me and our child in this world alone."

"I understand, sweetheart, and don't worry because I have no intentions on dying anytime soon," he replied, giving me that cocky ass smile of his.

The arrogance of this man drove me crazy sometimes, but one thing that I'd learned about Kwan since fate had brought us together in Los Angeles was not to underestimate him.

"That's a smart decision because if you die, I'm *definitely* gonna kill your ass when we meet in the next life. Now tell me how long you're gonna be gone."

He laughed softly as he stood up and pulled me to my feet with him. "This shit should only take a couple days, maybe a week at most. Don't worry, lil mama, I'll check in on you and our baby," he said, putting his hand on my stomach.

"Oh, I know that you will, and you'll do it *every* single day or I'ma be back stateside before you know it," I vowed, giving him a pointed look so that he'd know my threat was no joke.

He nodded before he kissed me on the forehead and took my hand while pulling me from the room.

"Wait, what about my food?" I asked, looking over my shoulder longingly at the tray still sitting on the bed.

His laughter was instant and loud, causing me to smack him in the back as I pulled free of his grip and went back to get my food.

"I'm smart enough not to criticize your appetite," he said, still chuckling.

"Good to know."

Once I'd grabbed the tray, I followed him out and into the kitchen where the sounds of voices were coming from. The first thing I saw was Tink's naked ass standing at the stove cooking.

"Bitch, I know you lying! What are you doing cooking?" I asked, more than a little surprised.

"You say that like I can't cook, bitch, but you know damn well that I know my way around the kitchen," she replied defensively.

"That ain't no lie," Jayson said around a mouthful of food.

The fact that we were all in the kitchen naked spoke to how comfortable we'd gotten sharing this space, even though we were on a yacht and not a small fishing boat. I sat down across from Jayson, but he didn't stay long because Kwan pulled him up by his arm and they disappeared out to the back deck.

"What's going on?" Tink asked, sitting beside me with her own plate of food.

"It's a long story."

"I'm sure, but I'ma need you to give me the short, bittersweet version," she replied.

"Skii called to tell me that my dad is looking for me."

Tink sat quietly for a moment, but I could feel her thinking loudly. "For Skii to hear about it means that he's not asking casual questions, and you know what that means for a nigga like Uncle Kenny," she said, looking over at me.

"I know...Kwan is gonna handle it."

"Meaning what?"

"He's not gonna kill him; he's just gonna stop him from coming after us," I said looking at her.

"Maybe he should. I mean I love your dad as much as you do, but I fear for the life of my unborn child. If you don't then you're not being realistic about how savage and ruthless your dad can be. At some point you're gonna have to choose, and it's gonna be his life...or ours."

Chapter 3

Kwan

NYC
2 days later

"Bruh, you do realize that it's damn near winter here, right?" Jayson asked, wrapping both hands around his Starbucks cup.

"What's your point?"

"My point is that you could've left my black ass on the yacht enjoying the sunshine and sea breeze," he replied.

"You sound cranky, my nigga. Do you need a nap?" I asked, chuckling softly as I lifted my Starbucks cup to my lips.

His response was to throw his middle finger up at me, and I knew that this was his way of keeping shit cute because we were in a public place.

"Don't worry, we'll be back on vacation just as soon as we handle the business that brought us back here," I said.

"Speaking of which, where the hell are Fabian and Blaze?"

I'd been wondering the same thing because we'd been waiting on them for half an hour, but just as I was getting ready to verbalize this, I saw both men coming through the front door.

"They're here," I said, nodding in their direction.

Jayson didn't bother to turn around and look; he just scooted around in the booth that we were occupying to make room for them. When they got to the table, they both sat down without saying anything.

"Took you niggas long enough," Jayson said.

"Aww, I missed you too," Blaze replied sarcastically.

"I almost did, but you niggas didn't stay gone long enough," Fabian said, smirking.

"You niggas cost me $100k because I bet on the over/under for how long good pussy could keep you both domesticated, and I thought that you'd at least last six months," Blaze said, shaking his head.

Fabian's laughter made it obvious who collected the $100k.

"Trust me when I tell you that we'd still be laid up in good pussy if it wasn't absolutely necessary for us to come back outside," I said seriously.

The laughter immediately dried up, and I could tell that I had their attention.

"You didn't give us any details, so what's up?" Fabian asked.

"My father-in-law has been trying to find out our whereabouts, and he's asking these questions in a way that's concerning," I replied.

"What do you mean?" Blaze asked.

"Well, Kyndra got a call from Skylar's little sister who let her know that she'd heard that Big Hands was looking for her. Skylar's sister is a wiz with a computer like her late sister was, and she keeps her ears to the street, which means that her hearing about the inquiries being made came from underground. We're too respected and feared in the underground not to have heard about this, unless that nigga was using his influence to try and keep shit quiet. That concerns me," I said.

"Not to mention the fact that we spared his life once, and he should already know that we don't give second chances," Jayson added.

"*okay*, hold up. You said that Skylar's sister is a hacker? What's her name because we need to make sure that her info is solid," Fabian said.

"Her name is Skii," I replied.

The visible response on Fabian's face told me that he was, at the very least, aware of her name.

"I take it that you've heard of her in your circles," Jayson said.

"Yeah, in the cyber circles she's known as Skii High, and she's got skills. She shut down half of Canada's power grid just because she didn't like the way that Drake talked about Kendrick Lamar," Fabian said, with clear admiration for what Skii could do.

"*okay* well since you know her, you can reach out to her and validate the threat, but in the meantime we've been working on a plan," I said.

Blaze and Fabian exchanged a quick look, but neither of them said anything.

"If you're thinking that we should just kill this nigga and be done with it, then we're in agreement with you. It's more complicated than that though," Jayson said.

"So much more complicated," I agreed.

"Okay, so what's the play?" Blaze asked, leaning closer so that our voices could be kept low.

"Well, I view Kyndra's dad as nothing more than a piece to be moved off of life's chessboard, but it can't be done by any of us because we don't know exactly who he has in his pockets. Where there's one fed, there's sure to be more, and I'm not trying to kill any more of them right now," I said.

"*okay*, so who do we get to do our dirty work?" Fabian asked curiously.

"The Chinese Triad," Jayson replied.

The confusion on Blaze and Fabian's faces was evident, but neither I nor Jayson said anything because we knew they'd figure it out sooner than later.

"Where is Big Hands now?" Blaze asked.

"Lower Manhattan," I replied.

"Where are we planting the pieces that we lifted in LA, and how much are we actually about to give up?" Fabian asked.

Jayson and I shared a look that morphed into a smile because our niggas were as sharp as ever.

"Of course we're not coming off of anything *near* all of what we took. Just enough to make the Triad believe that Big Hands orchestrated the jack move," I said.

"*okay*, but don't you think that he's gonna tell them that it was really us that masterminded and carried out that heist?" Blaze asked.

"Of course he will, but they won't believe him because we'll be the ones implicating him when we willingly turn over some of the stolen loot. We're just respectable businessmen that collect art," Jayson said.

"*okay*, so give me the numbers. Exactly how much are we planning on parting with in total?" Fabian asked again.

"Fifteen percent, roughly, which still leaves enough missing to torture and kill for," I said, smiling.

I watched as my niggas absorbed the idea of losing money because I knew firsthand that this wasn't how we typically played shit. It was necessary to use misdirection in this situation though, and in the end we'd actually be alive to reap the fruits of our labors.

"It's gonna take at least a few days to put this shit together, especially because it makes the most sense to stash the artifacts at the house Big Hands has in New Jersey. I'll need to pull the layout and check the security he has in place because it's sure to be top of the line," Fabian said.

"That sounds about right," Jayson said.

"Why don't you recruit Skii to help you, since she's more or less extended family," I suggested.

"Do you think that's smart considering what happened to Skylar?" Jayson asked, looking over at me.

"We're covered when it comes to Skylar, and Kyndra damn sure ain't saying shit," I replied.

The three of them shared a look, but none of them spoke up to question my decision with regards to trusting my wife. That was definitely a smart move on their part.

"How do you plan on making contact with the Triad?" Blaze asked.

"Through one of the brokers that we've used to move stolen merchandise before," I replied.

"I'll be taking care of that part, as well as taking care of the next job we're gonna pull off," Jayson said.

"What job?" Fabian asked, narrowing his gaze.

I chuckled before sipping from my cup and responding.

"You didn't think that we'd simply eliminate Big Hands, did you?" I asked.

"The way we figured it, that nigga gotta have a helluva piggy bank that he's not gonna need no more. So, we might as well get that up off him," Jayson said, smiling.

"That's that shit I'm talking 'bout," Blaze said, grinning and rubbing his hands together eagerly.

"Let me know when you need tech support," Fabian said.

"Just as soon as you finish outlining Big Hands' security setup, then you can jump straight into tracking his money and assets," I said.

Fabian nodded in understanding, and when I turned my eyes on Blaze, he did the same thing.

"Since we can't be gone from our significant others for too long, let's get this shit done quickly and painlessly," Jayson said.

"We gotchu," Blaze said, sliding out of the booth.

Fabian followed his lead, and within moments they were gone as quickly and quietly as they'd come.

"What's the next move?" Jayson asked.

"Well, while you do what you do, I'ma slide out to check on Rashawna."

"Do you think it's a good idea?" he asked, eyeing me closely.

"I mean, yeah. I ain't talked to her for real since we left except to check in by text message every now and then. We need a face-to-face convo so that I can tell her that I took care of the person responsible for her losing our child," I replied.

"Are you ready to have that conversation?"

"I gotta be because she deserves some type of closure," I said, sliding out of the booth and pulling some cash from my pocket.

I dropped a $20 bill on the table before pulling out my phone to text Rashawna to let her know that I was on my way to see her.

"You cool with taking a cab?" I asked.

"Yeah, I'm good, bruh. I'ma go back to your spot and get some work done."

"Cool. Keep your eyes open because if that nigga Big Hands knows that you're back in NYC, he might try to make a move on you," I warned.

"You already know that I'll drop that nigga where he stands," Jayson said, climbing out of the booth and handing me the key fob to the black Mercedes McLaren sitting out front.

"I'll call you when I'm on my way back."

He nodded, and I headed for the front door. After a brief battle with the strong wind, I slid behind the wheel of the sleek sports car and pulled off into the swiftly moving traffic. It took me almost half an hour to reach open highway where I could let the power and speed of the McLaren eat up the road. As the miles raced past, I let my mind wander to the impending conversation, trying to formulate the right words, and before I knew it, I was pulling up to Rashawna's townhouse in Northwest D.C. I sat there for a good five minutes, until she pulled her front door open and stood there looking very much impatient. I was just happy that she had clothes on this time. After two deep breaths, I climbed out of the car and went to face the music.

"Well, look who's back from the dead," she said sarcastically.

"It's good to see you too."

I opened my arms for a hug, but instead of her stepping into my arms as expected, she fired a swift jab that connected with my mouth before I could block it.

"Yo, what the fuck, Shawna?" I yelled, taking a step back.

"You know that you had that shit coming, so shut up. You can hug me now," she said, opening her arms and smiling.

I could taste the blood in my mouth, and that shit had me seeing red, but I damn sure wasn't about to hit her back.

"You're lucky that I love your crazy ass."

"Right back at you, my nigga," she said, pulling me into her arms and then leading me into the house.

We went into the living room and sat on the couch.

"You want some ice for your lip?" she asked, stroking the side of my face lovingly.

"If this is your way of saying that you missed me, then I'd rather you just smoke one with a nigga or something."

She chuckled ruefully and leaned her head against my shoulder.

"Of course I missed your muthafuckin ass! I'm not sorry for punching you in your shit though because it was a dick move for you to disappear on me. I get it though," she said.

"I'm sorry... shit got hectic though," I replied.

Neither of us spoke for a few minutes, but I felt the question coming.

"So... did you get 'em?" she asked softly.

"Dismembered and boiled in acid."

"Oh god, that's graphic," she said.

"Yeah, but I wanted you to know that she suffered before leaving this earth."

I heard the sound of her breathing change, and I knew she was crying, so I wrapped my arms around her and let her grieve. We stayed like that for a long while, and once she'd pulled herself together, she sat up to grab a half-smoked blunt from the ashtray.

"You want some?" she asked, lighting it and reclaiming her position in my arms.

I hit the blunt twice when she held it to my lips, holding the smoke until my lungs felt scorched before letting it out.

"It's good."

"I know. I invested in a new dispensary while you were gone," she replied before hitting the blunt again.

"How's the restaurant doing?"

"It's doing well. It was hard for me to go back there for *awhile*, but lucky for me, I'd hired some very *capable* people," she said.

"Look at you turning into a full-blown *businesswoman*," I said, admiring her hustle and drive.

"I'm just getting a head start on my second act in life because I'm not sure how much longer I wanna be a *judge*."

Hearing this came as a surprise to me because I'd always thought that she loved being a *judge*.

"You know that I'll support you in any way that you need," I said sincerely.

"I'm glad that you said that because I need to ask something of you, and it's a *big* deal," she said, passing me the blunt.

I instantly felt my nerves stand up as my internal warning system started ringing in my ears. I didn't say anything until after I'd finished the blunt off and tossed the roach in the ashtray. I was definitely feeling the high coming on, which made me relax somewhat and remember that Rashawna was a woman I could trust.

"Talk to me. How much do you need?"

"It's not money that I need from you; it's something a little more...*personal*," she replied evasively.

"That sounds like you need someone to *disappear*."

"No, nothing so *dramatic*. I just need some of your sperm," she said nonchalantly.

"You need...what?" I asked, looking down at her and wondering just how high she was.

"Your sperm. I need your sperm so I can get pregnant again."

"Sweetheart, you know that's not gonna bring our baby back," I said gently.

"Yeah, I know that, but it'll help heal the *hole* in my heart."

The vulnerability in her voice pulled at my soul and my conscience, but in my mind's eye, I was seeing my wife's face, and there was no way I could explain this to her.

"Shawna, you know things are different now because I'm married."

"I get that, but your wife doesn't ever have to know. It'll be our secret, and you know I'm good at keeping secrets. I *need this*, Kwan...so will you do it for me? Will you get me pregnant?"

Chapter 4

Kyndra

"You want another nonalcoholic strawberry daiquiri?" Tink asked.

"Not unless you're adding some rum to that muthafucka."

She laughed as she sat down on the lounge chair next to mine on the yacht's upper deck, but I was so not joking. I missed my nigga so bad it would drive a bitch to drink, smoke, and *shoot* a bitch for looking at me wrong. I knew this was *irrational*, and it was just my pregnancy hormones kicking my ass. It felt so much *deeper* though.

"I miss my man too, cuz, so don't feel too bad."

"I don't feel bad, I feel fucking *crazy*!" I admitted.

"I know what you mean. It's hard as fuck to sleep in bed without having Jayson wrapped around me, and I don't like it because I ain't never been a bitch who was pressed 'bout no man. Shit definitely hits *different* when it comes to Jayson though."

"Yeah, I know what you mean. It's like I wanna be in that nigga Kwan's skin," I said, shaking my head in disgust with myself.

Tink laughed, but she was nodding in agreement and understanding.

"I didn't never imagine being *open* like this behind a man. We've even been talking about *marriage*," she confessed.

I knew my surprise must've been written all over my face because she laughed again and blushed at the same time.

"I won't lie to you, *marriage* is a big deal. I love this shit though. I love knowing I've found my person to walk through life with, and it's only fitting that he's a certified Jackboy," I replied.

"Right! I never imagined I'd find a nigga to love who was as *deep* in the game as we are!"

"I ain't gonna lie, I feel like them niggas is *deeper* in the game than us, but bitch, that shit is so muthafuckin *sexy!*" I said, laughing as I high-fived her.

"Have you and Kwan shared war stories yet?"

"Not really, just the job in LA they pulled off flawlessly. Of course, they know about our move against the cartel," I replied.

"That muthafuckin move they pulled in LA was *masterful,* and once I knew Jayson was part of that, I swear I tried to suck the skin off that nigga's dick," she bragged, without shame.

I laughed until my stomach hurt, but only because I knew exactly how she felt. There was something about knowing the criminal *genius* of Kwan that put me on my *fifty shades of grey meets mardi graz* crossed with Atlanta's infamous *Freaknik.* Behind closed doors I was my man's slut puppy, and I *loved* it.

"That type of energy is gonna have your crazy ass pregnant every year," I warned.

"I don't give a fuck because these pussy walls still gonna put the *death grip* on that muthafuckin dick."

"Facts, bitch, *facts!*" I said, laughing with her.

Our laughter was interrupted by her phone pinging with a notification, and I could tell by the shit-eating grin on her face that the message was from Jayson.

"Damn, Tink, at least *try* to hide some of your teeth, bitch."

"Bitch, fuck you, because you be the same way when it comes to Kwan."

I knew she was telling the truth, so I kept my mouth shut and picked up my own phone. I'd intended to play around on social media, but I quickly found myself rereading old texts from Kwan while fighting the urge to message him now. My willpower lasted all of thirty seconds, and then my thumbs were working furiously, sending what I prayed sounded like an innocent text. I wasn't trying to be clingy, but damn I missed him. It felt like I was holding my breath for five minutes, but in reality it was a hot thirty seconds before he hit me back with the loving words of affirmation I was craving.

"I see that shit-eating grin on your face, bitch," Tink said, chuckling.

"Man, fuck you."

I laughed with her as I closed out my messages and hopped on Facebook. As soon as I saw I had a message from Skii, my smile faltered because I figured it was more bad news. Surprisingly, she wanted my advice about one of the niggas in Kwan's crew who'd reached out to her.

"Tink, what do you know about Fabian?"

"Kwan and Jayson's people?" she asked.

"Yeah, him."

"Not much, just that he's family and the third man in their four-man crew. I think the other nigga is named Blaze, but they both seemed cool when we worked together moving the cartel stash. Why do you ask?" she asked, looking over at me.

"Because Skii just hit me up and wanted to know what I thought."

"That makes sense because Fabian is the *hacker* in the crew," she said, nodding.

"Okay, well apparently he wants her to work with them on some shit," I said, already typing a message back to Skii.

"So we're joining forces now? *'Bout time*, but damn, why we gotta be on the *sideline*?"

I could hear the disappointment in her voice, and I felt a twinge of it myself, but after everything that had happened to Kwan, I wasn't putting our baby in danger.

"We won't be sidelined *indefinitely*. Trust me, our niggas know we're working women, and we'll be working moms," I said.

"You think Jayson and Kwan will go for that when the time comes?"

"Yeah. They're undoubtedly attracted to that part of us, just like we are to them," I replied, finishing my message to Skii.

"Makes sense… but I won't lie to you, cuz, I've thought about retiring and being a *stay-at-home mom*," she confessed.

"I get it, and I've thought about the same thing since that night I found you sitting in the *dark* on my balcony in Santorini. What happened after that definitely made me want to retire, but the life of a jackgirl sings to me like a *succubus* luring me into the darkness. We've been doing this shit for so long I can't see just quitting and being a *home body*."

"You think we'll be good mothers?" she asked softly.

Her question made me think about both our mothers, and that definitely wasn't a road I was ready to go down.

"We're gonna be great moms, cuz. Don't worry about that. And we'll always have each other to lean on," I vowed sincerely.

Her phone rang before she could reply, and she got up while answering, which told me it was Jayson calling. My fingers were itching again, but I resisted the temptation because I could see Skii typing me another message. I thought she was coming for more sisterly advice about Fabian, but instead she dropped the bomb that my father was still looking for me. Instead of feeling fear, I was *annoyed*, and that quickly morphed into *anger*. Before I knew it, I was dialing his number, and it was ringing in my ear. I wasn't worried about him tracking my location because I still had the encrypted phone Kwan had given me.

"Who is this?" asked a gruff voice I recognized.

"It's the person you're so desperate to find. Now, what the fuck do you want?"

"Who is this?" he asked again, trying to play dumb.

"Father, cut the *bullshit* and tell me what the fuck you want," I demanded, anger rising.

"You know *exactly* what the fuck I want, you ungrateful little bitch!"

"Ungrateful? Nigga, didn't I save your miserable fucking life when I could've very easily deaded you?" I yelled, feeling my blood immediately start to boil.

"You forget your place, Kyndra, and going against me is as *futile* as warring with God Almighty. You really believe that JaKwan can protect you or keep you hidden from me forever? Are you *really* that naïve?"

"I'm far from naïve, old nigga. I'm just supremely confident my nigga will body you if you keep playing," I said.

His laughter echoing across the phone line made my skin crawl and only pissed me off more. I was definitely regretting not shooting him when I had the chance.

"It's so *cute* that you really believe you know the nigga you're married to. You have no *idea* what enemy you're sleeping with."

"Is this your pathetic attempt to turn me against my husband?" I asked, chuckling humorlessly.

"I wouldn't dream of turning you against him, because in the end he'll destroy you for me, and the blood won't be on my hands. I'm just trying to make sure I get my *property* back before your untimely murder…or suicide."

His last comment turned my blood cold as I felt the knife in my chest twist under his grip. No one knew better than my father why the thought of suicide paralyzed me, and the fact that he so casually threw it at me showed just how *evil* he truly was.

"I would say I hope you rot in *hell*, but honestly? I'm praying to God there's something worse than hell waiting for you. You deserve it," I said, disconnecting the call before he could do more damage.

I wanted to hurl my phone into the ocean, but my self-control made me simply drop it onto the deck. I could feel the tears streaming down my face, and I was pissed at myself for letting him upset me so badly. The more I swiped at the wetness on my face, the more the tears fell, and I finally gave in to the inevitable sobs ripping out of my vocal cords. I'd always known how cruel my father could be, but I'd never had that cruelty directed at me with so much blatant hatred. The fact that our relationship had deteriorated to this point was more than surprising because I'd grown up a daddy's girl. Now I was the *opp*, and he'd done everything he could to make sure I felt that way. What I really felt was sick to my stomach, and I knew if I kept crying I was gonna end up vomiting everywhere.

"Whoa, whoa, whoa, what's wrong?" Tink asked, sounding panicked.

When I looked up, I saw her rushing toward me, and I opened my arms for her to climb into the lounge chair with me. It took me another five minutes of uncontrollable crying before I finally pulled my shit together enough to talk.

"I—I called my dad," I mumbled.

"Oh."

Her one-word response told me she understood what happened without me getting into the details, and I was grateful not to have to relive his *viciousness*. Tink held me close, and my tears eventually subsided completely, even though I was left emotionally exhausted and physically weak. I couldn't remember being this upset since I was little and my biological mother had died. This situation was similar because I was grieving the relationship I'd lost with my last living parent, but I knew there was no *shortcut* to dealing with grief. In a lot of ways, I needed to feel this pain and completely detach myself from that man.

"Thanks, Tink," I said, grateful that she'd been here.

"You've done the same for me, so there's no need to thank me. Do you wanna talk about what happened?"

"No, because it doesn't matter. I'm done with him," I vowed sincerely.

"Well, you already know I'm with you no matter what."

I nodded and kissed her forehead in gratitude.

"Do me a favor and hand me my phone, please," I said.

She got up off the lounge chair and looked around until she located it on the deck. Once she handed it back to me, I sent Kwan a message that consisted of two words: *destroy him*. I didn't feel better about campaigning my own father's *demise*, but I wasn't sorry, and I wouldn't have any regrets.

"Excuse me, Miss Kyndra, but I just received radio traffic from your *sentries* on the water informing me that we need to move because a U.S. warship has entered these international waters," the Captain said from a few feet away.

A knot immediately formed in the pit of my stomach because I didn't believe in *coincidence*, and the fact that I'd just spoken to my father was at the forefront of my mind.

"How far away is the ship?" I asked calmly.

"I'm not sure, ma'am, but it's not yet within sight of us, so my best guess is that it's still around the point," he replied.

"Okay, take us around the coast of Africa, and if the ship follows us then we'll sail into port and get off. Make sure you raise the Moroccan flag so if they deploy drones, they'll think this yacht belongs to locals," I said, standing up.

"Very good, Miss Kyndra," he replied as he turned and left.

"You think it's your dad?" Tink asked, sensing my thoughts.

"You know like I do that there's no such thing as *coincidence*. It might not be him, but either way we don't need to be spotted by an American *military* ship, because we don't know how far my father's reach is. If he even gets word of our possible location, he'd send his goons."

"I get it. Where are we going though?" she asked.

"We're both going below deck so we aren't seen," I replied, taking her hand in mine and leading the way.

Once we were secured inside with the sliding glass door that accessed the back deck closed, I felt a little better—but not much. I was more than tempted to call Kwan, but I knew he had enough on his plate. Instead, I decided to text the one person I knew could get equally quick results. I sat on the couch and sent Skii a message asking her to hack the United States Department of Defense and find out why they had a U.S. destroyer near Africa. She hit me back immediately with a thumbs-up emoji, and then it was just a waiting game. I wasn't trying to go to war with the U.S. *military*, so I wouldn't make any unprovoked moves, but I would defend myself, my cousin, and our unborn children.

"Tink, tell the Captain to ready the RPGs we have onboard, just in case."

"You think it'll come to that?" she asked, looking concerned.

"I don't know, cuz, but if they start a fight, then we're gonna be as *ready* as possible. For our kids' sake."

Chapter 5

Kwan

The buzzing of my phone interrupted our conversation momentarily, but I sent Kyndra a text back before returning my attention to Rashawna.

"Do you need an answer right this moment?" I asked.

"It would be nice, considering I'm trying to get pregnant again as soon as possible. I've already been to the doctor for a thorough *checkup* to make sure there wouldn't be any *difficulties* with me getting pregnant or carrying a baby to term because of the shooting. I was given a clean bill of *health*, so all I really need is you," she replied, looking at me steadily.

It was on the tip of my tongue to ask why it had to be me who got her pregnant, but I already knew the *answer*.

"Shawna, I don't wanna be a *nothing ass* father to our child, but you know I'm married…so how do you envision this working?"

"You wouldn't be a *nothing ass* father because I know you'd come see me when you could, and I wouldn't put more *demands* on you than that. My expectations would be *realistic* to the situation, and I completely understand that you're married," she replied.

If I'd heard this from any other woman, I'd have serious difficulty believing it, but I knew that Rashawna knew how to play her *position*. I knew I could trust her. The question was—could I trust myself to balance what would essentially be two different lives? Because there would be no room for *error*.

"This will work, Kwan…just have a little *faith*," she said softly, placing her hand on my cheek.

Before I could say anything, she leaned up to kiss me. I was always lost in the softness of her juicy lips, and this time was no different. I felt the heat of our lust sucking the oxygen from the room, pushing us dangerously closer to an *inferno* neither of us could outrun. When she pulled back, I thought she was having second thoughts—but instead, she stood up from the couch and held her hand out to me. I hesitated for a few seconds before taking her hand, standing up, and letting her lead the way upstairs to her bedroom. Despite all the sexual encounters we'd had before, I felt butterflies in my stomach because this was different. We weren't fucking for sport—we were trying to make a baby.

"Take your clothes off," she demanded in a husky tone.

I did as I was told, and she watched with eyes filling with *anger* and *need* with each piece of clothing shed.

"I see someone's been working out," she said, smiling.

"Just a little something."

"Baby, there's *nothing* little about you," she said, quickly shedding her own clothes.

When she was naked, she pushed me back onto the bed and mounted me like a jockey at the Derby. I barely had time to appreciate her nakedness above me before she took my hard dick inside her and slid down that muthafucka like a fireman's pole. Her pussy was so tight and hot I would've bet all my money she hadn't fucked anyone since me. Her wetness combined with the grip of her walls gave her pussy the feeling of a Jacuzzi with suction jets. She kept her hands on my chest, which let her control the speed she rode with and how much dick she was willing to take. It was obvious she was determined—and that shit was sexy as fuck. I let her have her way for a moment, but then I began lifting my hips into her downward force, causing a seismic collision that made her beautiful eyes roll.

"Sh-shit, wait," she mumbled.

I ignored her weak plea, taking hold of her hips and gripping her tightly while increasing the force of my thrusts. Her expression morphed through different phases of *pleasurable passion* as she rode me like a mechanical bull in a bar full of people cheering her on. It only took a few minutes for her first orgasm to rip through her, causing her to scream my name with unrestrained *passion* that was as motivating as it was erotic. Before her body could stop trembling, I flipped her onto her back, pushed her knees up into her chest, and drove my dick back inside her from that angle.

"Oh God, Kwan," she moaned, sounding like it hurt so *good*.

The deeper I drove inside her, the more her pussy juices splashed up my shaft, creating an echoing sound of wetness that was *hypnotic*. I fucked her harder, knowing she could take dick like it was her favorite profession. Her pussy's grip was tighter than a pair of Vans without the strings, but I fought back like my ass was against the ropes in a 12-round fight.

I felt my desire to cum right around the corner, and I chased it like a dog chasing a fast-moving car. The feeling of her body going through its gears was obvious and familiar, so I waited until I knew she was ready to blow her engine before I wrecked us both.

"You...you...you seem m-motivated," she panted, giggling breathlessly.

"Making it *count*," I panted, easing my dick out of her and laying down beside her.

Neither of us spoke for a few moments because we were too busy sucking in oxygen and letting our bodies cool down.

"How long can you stay?" she asked.

I knew all the plans weren't in place for the moves we intended to make against Kyndra's father—and once that kicked off, there was no telling how long I'd be unavailable.

"We've got *time*."

"Then I suggest you get some water, because I definitely ain't had *enough*," she said, reaching over and stroking my dick lovingly.

I chuckled, but I got up and went into the bathroom to take her advice. When I came back out, she was sitting on the bed with several toys laid out beside her.

"You wanna have some *fun?*" she asked, smiling mischievously.

I laughed, but I definitely made my way over to her. From that point on, we spent the rest of the afternoon and into the early evening trying to fuck and suck each other's brains out. By the time it was over, I'd never been so thoroughly used in my life, and the smile on my face felt permanent.

"I'm gonna order us something to eat—do you have any *preferences?*" she asked.

"I'm kinda full from all the pussy I ate, but I can still do a steak and cheese."

"You're *stupid*," she said, laughing as she rolled over and grabbed her phone off the nightstand.

While she did that, I got up and retrieved my own phone from my pants on the floor, knowing I'd missed more than a few calls. Luckily none were from Kyndra—just Jayson and Fabian. I hit Jayson back first because he'd sent three text messages along with his calls.

"What's good, bruh?"

"Damn, nigga, I was wondering if Rashawna killed you for real this time," he replied.

"Trust me, she tried. What's up though—everything in motion?"

"For the most part, yeah, but some shit happened you're not gonna like," he said.

I felt the instant shift in my stomach, but I made sure to check my temper before it could take over and cloud my *vision*.

"What happened?" I asked calmly.

Chapter 6

Kyndra

"Tink hit me up and said that Kyndra had spoken to her father. Tink wasn't exactly sure what was said because she was on the phone with me in our bed when it happened, but she found Kyndra crying so hard she thought it was a *panic attack*."

I could feel my jaw clenching so hard I knew it would hurt later, but I kept my mouth shut until I was sure I wouldn't click the fuck out.

"I didn't get any calls from Kyndra. Is she alright?" I asked.

"Yeah, she's *good* now. And the reason she didn't call you was because she didn't want you to change your plans and go at her father with *guns blazing*."

Of course she would know the dangers of being controlled by your emotions in a life-or-death situation. Still, I felt some type of way that she hadn't called me for the emotional support she clearly needed. I also felt guilty, because if she *had* called me, I still would've missed it because of what I'd been doing.

"I'm on my way back to New York," I said, hanging up before he could respond.

"Is everything okay?" Rashawna asked from behind me.

"No."

I didn't elaborate. I just put my clothes on while wrestling with the emotions warring inside me. When I was dressed, I went to her side of the bed and leaned in to place a gentle kiss on her forehead.

"I'll call you," I said.

"You better not get yourself killed, JaKwan, and I ain't fucking joking."

"Don't worry. Somebody's gonna die—but it ain't gonna be me," I replied as I turned to leave.

Within minutes, I was behind the wheel of the McLaren, speeding into the descending nightfall. I was mentally envisioning the different ways I could strip the flesh from a nigga's bones, and that kept my foot heavy on the gas pedal. I made it back to my spot in four hours flat, and I walked in to find my brother cooking.

"What the hell are you doing?" I asked, surprised.

"Trying out this new recipe Tink and I were talking about."

The absurdity of how uncharacteristic this was for him made me pause for a second just to make sure I'd heard him right. After that, I couldn't help laughing as I pulled out my phone.

"What the hell are *you* doing?" he asked, glaring at me.

"Man, you know Fabian and Blaze ain't gonna believe this shit unless they see it," I replied, recording him.

"Bruh, fuck you."

I kept right on laughing as I filmed him for a straight minute, then I got back to business.

"So, did you find out any more about the call between Kyndra and her father?" I asked.

"Nah. Tink ain't pushing the issue, which is probably smart based on how she described Kyndra's response. It scared Tink, because she automatically thought that with the way Kyndra was crying, something had happened to you."

"That means it was real *bad*," I said, pulling out a stool and sitting at the island in the kitchen.

"Yeah, that's what I was thinking—and wait a *minute*! Nigga, you smell like thirty-one flavors of pussy! What the fuck?" he exclaimed, stopping across from me.

"It's a long story."

"Make it a *short* one," he demanded.

"Rashawna wants another baby, and I understand because of what we lost. I also feel responsible for that loss, so I felt obligated to give her what she wanted," I replied honestly.

I could tell by the look on his face that he had an opinion about my actions, but he kept it to himself and went back to cooking.

"So where we at?" I asked, shifting back to business.

"Everything is in motion. The broker already has a couple of the pieces from the exhibit, with *bread crumbs* that lead back to Big Hands. Fabian liquidated his assets, so it's only a matter of time before he knows he's under attack."

"By that time the Triad should be breathing down his neck. Did you make sure they know we brought this to them? Because you know he's gonna give us up as the real culprits," I said.

"Yeah, we're good on that angle too. The only thing left is to find out where his emergency cash is, because we know he's too smart not to have some rainy-day money."

"Check all the usual spots offshore and in Switzerland. I'll see what Kyndra knows," I said, pulling my phone out and texting her.

"Okay, I'll have Fabian put Skii on it. He said she's even better than advertised."

"Sounds like *nerd flirting*," I said, chuckling softly.

"Probably—but I ain't knocking it. Taste this," he said, holding out a spoon with some red sauce on it.

I complied and was surprised at how good it was.

"Mmm…just the right amount of salt. What's it go with?"

"It goes over tortellini pasta with Italian sausage and a side Caesar salad," he replied, rinsing the spoon and going back to the stove.

"I ain't mad at that."

"I *am* mad at how you smell. Go take a shower and rest up for a few hours, because you look like Rashawna ain't let you sleep," he said over his shoulder.

I started to say some smart shit, but he was right all the way around, so I kept my mouth shut. I left him to his culinary therapy and went upstairs to hop in the shower. After half an hour under the blistering spray of hot water, my body felt relaxed, and when I laid down I knew sleep was close. I didn't even remember falling asleep completely, but the sound of my phone chirping woke me up, and I was surprised to see sunlight filling my room.

I reached for the phone on my nightstand, expecting a message from my wife—but instead, I'd received a video message from a blocked number. The sleep left my body instantly, and I hopped up to go find Jayson. He was in the guest room, knocked the fuck out, but as soon as I walked in, he sat bolt upright with his gun in hand.

"Chill, it's me," I said.

"What's going on?" he asked groggily.

"How the fuck can someone send me an anonymous message to an *encrypted* phone?"

He wiped his eyes and swung his feet to the floor before looking over at me.

"What does the message say?" he asked.

"I don't know. It's a video."

We were both quiet for a moment, no doubt contemplating whatever was behind door number two in this house of horrors.

"Send it to Fabian first and let him go over it," he said.

"Good thinking."

Before I could forward the video or even send him a message to let him know it was coming, my phone started ringing in my hand.

"I was just about to hit you up," I said, answering and seeing Fabian's image on the screen.

"Did you get the video I sent?" he asked.

"That was you? Why the fuck does it say it came from a *blocked* number?" I asked.

"Because of where I got it from, but that don't matter. What matters is what's on the video—and you need to watch it ASAP."

"Okay, I'll call you back," I said, disconnecting.

Jayson hadn't moved but was staring at me with an expectant look, like he was impatient as hell for me to open the video.

I didn't know what to expect—and at first I was confused—but then it clicked.

"Mutha*fucka*!" I growled through clenched teeth.

"What is it?" Jayson asked.

I turned the phone toward him and replayed the clip.

"Ooooh…shit," he said softly.

"If this goes public, we've got a serious fucking *problem*."

"You think?" he asked sarcastically.

I could tell by his tone he was blaming me, and I couldn't even fault him—even though it wasn't helping.

"This has to be handled *immediately*, so get up and get dressed. We gotta kill everyone who's laid eyes on this video."

When two of the onboard crew members came into the room carrying surface-to-air RPG missiles, I instructed them to lay them on the floor in front of the couch.

"This shit is *crazy*," Tink said.

"I agree, but we really don't know what's going on," I replied.

"Do you want me to text Jayson?"

I thought about it for a moment, because I knew part of my father's diabolical plan could be to split our focus in order to divide us. I couldn't let that happen.

"We don't contact them until we know there's a reason to. I've got Skii hacking the Department of Defense to see if the warship has a legit reason for being out here. They could simply be patrolling the *shipping lanes* to discourage pirates," I said.

"True, they could be."

The look on her face told me she wasn't feeling this *wait and see* shit at all.

I knew it was probably because we were pregnant, and honestly, I didn't like it either for that reason. But it was *necessary* to play it like this, because when it came to the force of the United States military, you had to be absolutely sure that was the war you wanted.

I could already feel the yacht moving, which eased me a little. When my phone sounded off, I expected it to be Skii—but it was a message from Kwan asking if I knew where my father would hide his emergency money. I didn't even need to guess. I knew exactly where he kept his stash to run with, but knowing he was at war, he might've turned it into a setup.

"Is that Skii?" Tink asked.

"Nah, it's Kwan."

"Why you got that look on your face?" she asked.

"Because I'm trying to think like my father for a second."

"Okay, I'm REALLY gonna need you to explain that shit," she said, sounding more concerned.

"Kwan just asked me where my father would hide his emergency money. And I know where it is, but I'm wondering if it's a setup to go after it. My father could be anticipating that move simply because he knows he's at war with us—and we know a big part of his power is his money," I said.

"When you put it like that, I can see why Uncle Kenny would be anticipating that move. So what you gonna do?"

I thought for a moment, then texted Kwan my thoughts to get his perspective.

"Miss Kyndra, this radio traffic just came for you," a female crew member said, entering the parlor and handing me a piece of paper.

I read the message and gave her a curt nod. Once she left, I passed the note to Tink.

"Okay, so does this mean we overreacted?" she asked.

"No, it just means the warship stopped and dropped anchor. That could mean they know we're in the area but don't know exactly where. So for now, we keep moving as far from them as possible."

"I got you. Do you still think we're safer on the water than on land?" she asked.

"I don't know for real. This was a good idea as long as no one knew we were out here. But if my father and his associates start checking the oceans, there's only so much we can do to hide. Not to mention the President's *fondness* for blowing up boats and ships he thinks are smuggling drugs. Maybe it's time to hide among people," I replied.

"Where would we go?"

I'd given this question a lot of *thought* in the months since we first set sail, knowing we'd eventually have to rejoin society. I longed for the comfort and safety of our spot in Santorini, Greece, but we couldn't draw attention to that location because of the gold and platinum bars hidden there. It was easy to get lost in a major city like New York City, but that was my father's playground, and hiding in plain sight only worked in movies.

"I've been thinking about Tokyo," I said.

"Japan? What made you think about going there?" she asked, giving me a curious look.

"It's beautiful over there, and the culture is *diversified* because Americans have a big presence. It would be different, for sure."

"Yeah, I see what you're saying. I was thinking about claiming one of the islands in the Caribbean. We could blend in with the constant stream of tourists—or we could put our money together and buy our own island," she suggested.

I hadn't actually considered buying an island before, but it wasn't a bad idea. It would definitely offer the privacy we wanted, and the Somali pirates could still protect us by surrounding the island.

"That could cost between thirty and a hundred million, depending on how big the island is," I replied.

"Stop acting like we can't put that type of money together, you penny-pinching ass bitch."

"Oh, I know we can. I'm just making sure *you* understand the commitment—that shit ain't like owning a house or a car," I said.

"I feel you. It would be a dope-ass move though."

I nodded, but my attention was pulled back to my phone as another message came through.

"Skii said the U.S. warship is doing scheduled training exercises—and they were approved six months ago," I said, relieved.

"Tell that bitch I said she's a bad muthafucka to hack the U.S. Department of Defense so fast."

I laughed but sent the message, then texted Kwan again since he still hadn't responded. I knew he'd asked about the money because they were planning moves against my father—but I needed him to *think*. If he didn't respond soon, I'd start making plans for me and Tink to head back to the States, and I knew he didn't want that.

After a few minutes of staring at my phone, impatience got the better of me.

"Tink, text Jayson and ask him if Kwan is with him."

"I got you," she said, pulling her phone out and typing.

"Miss Kyndra, would you like me to return the RPGs to their spot below deck?" the female crew member asked, stepping inside.

"Please, and thanks," I replied, still distracted by thoughts of my husband.

I knew Kwan and his crew could handle anything, but I couldn't stop myself from worrying. This was the part of love I hated. When a few minutes passed with no reply from Jayson, I felt Tink's unease radiating.

"Maybe they're in the middle of *snatching* him," she said.

"I don't doubt that. I just need them not to do anything *stupid*."

"Cuz, you know them niggas is too smart for that," she said confidently.

Before I could voice my fear, my phone finally sounded off with a text—and seconds later, Tink's did too. When I read the message, my mouth dropped open and I had to swallow so I wouldn't choke on my own spit.

"Tell me these niggas got jokes," Tink said.

I didn't tell her that. I just clicked the video link and watched the shit unfold myself.

"This ain't a joke," I said immediately.

"Did you know your dad put cameras in his spot in New York?"

"Fuck no. But I suspect he did it to cover his ass because he was dealing with crooked government employees. It's smart—but right now it's got us fucked up because Kwan killed that Fed and we were all right there," I said.

"You think your dad knows Kwan knows about the video?"

"I doubt it. He sounded way too *cocky* when I talked to him. No doubt he thinks this is his *ace in the hole*. But I know my husband—and this shit is gonna make Kwan kill him *personally*," I said, already texting him back, telling him not to make impulsive decisions.

"What do you think your dad planned to do with the video? If he exposes us, he's gotta explain what he and Mr. Wheaton were up to," she said.

"Did you notice the video didn't come with *audio*? That gives dear old dad the opportunity to say he was having a *legit business meeting* we interrupted—and Kwan killed the Fed for no reason."

"Ohhh…shit," she mumbled.

"My thoughts exactly."

This time it didn't take long for Kwan to hit me back—but all he said was that *everything was under control* and I didn't need to worry.

I thought about accepting that at face value, but my heart knew he was trying to dumb shit down so I wouldn't stress myself or the baby. I needed the truth about how bad this was, so I sent Skii a message asking what she knew about the video.

While I waited, I tried to think of ways we could get out of this mess, and I had a feeling what it would take to make my father back off.

"All he really wants is what we jacked from the cartel," I said.

"Okay, and?"

"And maybe we should just *give it to him*, and he'll leave us alone," I replied.

"I'd love to believe that, but I know just how *unforgiving* your father is. This might've started behind that lick we pulled, but at the end of the day, you chose your nigga over him. Even though you spared his life, all he's gonna remember is your *betrayal*—and you know how he feels about people who betray him."

"He doesn't feel anything—'cause they're already dead to him," I said, understanding too well the point she was making.

I'd come too far to go back, and the way forward required bloodshed like a toll fee. This knowledge made the uneasiness in my stomach worse, because ultimately, I'd made the choice between Kwan and my father—and I needed Kwan not to get hurt.

When my phone rang in my hand, I expected Kwan's face to pop up—but it was Skii instead.

"What's up, sis?" I answered.

"Knee-deep in the game and *loving* it. Not to mention the fact that Fabian is fine as fuck too," she giggled.

"Stay focused, Skii. What's the deal with this video?"

"The video was hidden in your father's iCloud account, and I doubt he knows we hacked him. He can't get back into that account, so unless he has a copy stashed somewhere, everything should be good," she replied.

"Have you looked everywhere you can think of to see if he has a copy of it?"

"Of course, Kyndra, but if he's got a hard copy, we'd be looking for a needle in a stack of *needles*."

What she was saying made sense, and I tried to think of all the places my father would hide something like that. Its value was *priceless* to him, so it wouldn't be just laying around.

"Imma call you back, Skii," I said, disconnecting and turning to Tink.

"Why you looking at me like that?"

"Because I'm about to do something I shouldn't do—and you're coming with me," I replied.

"Mannnn…*shit*. Why you trying to get me into some shit with my future husband?" she asked, pouting.

"Because it's necessary to save all of us."

"I know I'm gonna regret asking this, but what is it you think we *need* to do?" she asked, exasperated.

"If my father has a copy of that video—and I'm sure he does—then it's more than likely at his house in New Jersey. He's about to have his hands full with Kwan and his crew, so this is the best opportunity for us to get to Jersey and get it," I explained.

"You think we just gonna walk in and walk out with no issues?"

"I didn't say that—but whatever issue pops up, we're just gonna have to *pop off* on."

I could read the indecision in her eyes, but I also saw the smirk. She missed the *action* as much as I did, even if neither of us said it out loud.

"Okay, so how do we pull this off?" she asked.

"We need to sneak back into the country, so we can either come through Canada or Mexico."

"We're not fugitives yet, so we don't gotta sneak around. Plus, we don't know when—or if—your dad's gonna retreat to his New Jersey fortress. We need to be in and out, then vanish like *smoke*," she said.

I gave her idea some thought before nodding decisively, then got back on the phone to arrange travel.

"This yacht has a helipad, so go tell the captain a helicopter will be landing just as fast as I can charter it," I said.

"I gotchu," she replied, leaving the room.

Luckily, the nearest charter was in Morocco, and I had the deal done within minutes. I wasn't comfortable keeping Kwan in the dark, but it was for the *greater good*. I just hoped he forgave me later.

"The captain says we're good to go," Tink said when she returned.

"Okay. We can't take the helicopter all the way back to the U.S., so we're gonna touch down in Morocco and fly private straight to Teterboro. I'll get a rental."

"What about weapons? 'Cause I damn sure ain't goin' in *unarmed*," she said.

Her point was valid, and I wasn't stepping into my father's house without big shit to protect us. The only solution was calling in a favor from some Brooklyn niggas I'd worked with before.

"I got it," I said, firing off a text.

"Okay, so I'm gonna put some clothes on."

"Yeah, me too—but you BETTER NOT let Jayson know what we're doing," I said with a stern look.

"Okay, damn, I hear you, bitch. Stop giving me the crazy eyes," she said, sucking her teeth as she walked out.

I wasn't questioning her loyalty on purpose, but I knew how torn *I* felt deceiving the man I loved. Neither of us had ever been in this position before—it had always been us and our crew against the world. But this love had *domesticated* us in ways we never expected.

I didn't fault Tink any more than I faulted myself—but this was about securing the future we all imagined. We all had dirt under our nails and blood on our hands, which meant we probably didn't deserve a happily ever after. That wasn't gonna stop me from chasing it—even if it meant adding more blood to my hands.

My father was right that I'd chosen my nigga over him— but it was more than that. I'd chosen *my future* over the life he planned for me.

That was a decision I'd live with…and die with.

And kill for.

Chapter 7

Kwan

My first thought was to run down on Big Hands while he was right here in NYC like a *knight* storming a castle, but the knowledge that he had cameras covering every square inch of his spot deterred me momentarily. After confirming with Fabian that the video was authentic, I'd reached out to the broker we'd given the stolen artifacts from the LA gallery heist and made sure he pointed the triad in the right direction. He assured me the triad now knew who was behind the robbery, and they were eager to get their hands on him so they could make an example out of him. I made sure to disclose he was in New York, but holed up in a spot with a lot of cameras.

Once that call was completed, I hit Blaze up and made sure he was up to speed on the latest events, then told him to find us a way inside Big Hands' place in lower Manhattan. While he was working on that, Jayson was calling in favors to get us a few mercenaries we could wind up and point at a muthafucka who needed killing. I'd told Kyndra not to worry because I didn't want her stressing in her condition, but the truth was that this situation could get out of control fast, and then we'd all be wanted fugitives. I'd dropped bodies before, obviously, but killing a fed came with a different set of problems. We wouldn't be wanted for questioning—they'd simply shoot to kill.

"Aight, bruh, I reached out to our Jamaican friends from Queens, and they're down to ride with us," Jayson said, coming into the home office.

"How many of them?"

"I figured we'd only need ten for what me and Blaze got planned," he said, taking a seat across from me at my desk.

"And what exactly do you have planned?" I asked.

"We attack from the top and bottom, using the sewer system that runs under Big Hands' spot."

"I'm not fucking around in no New York sewer, my nigga," I stated seriously.

He chuckled, but he knew damn well I meant what the fuck I said.

"There'll be explosives in place in the sewer beneath his house, and once they're detonated, it'll force him to run outside into our waiting arms."

"Okay, that sounds better. When do we kick the party off?"

"Right now I got the Jamaicans doing recon and planting the explosives, while Fabian and Skii keep tabs on what's going on inside because they're still tapped into his security system. I just checked with Fabian about ten minutes ago, and he said Big Hands is still in his spot in Manhattan enjoying a late lunch with a few white businessmen. Once I get word the explosives are in play, then you and I can move out to his location."

I nodded, already envisioning seeing my enemy dead at my feet. His daughter wasn't here to save his ass this time.

I stood up and walked over to a hidden compartment in the wall disguised as books, which required my retinal scan to open. Once it was open, I pulled out four AR-15s and two grenade launchers, stacking them in a chair beside me. I grabbed six extra clips and twelve grenades before closing the compartment and going to the hall closet for a duffel bag big enough to hold everything. Back in my office, I packed it up, then sat across from my brother again.

"What's on your mind, bruh?" he asked.

"What do you mean?"

"I know you better than anyone in the world, and I know when you got something on your mind. So what's up?"

I started to deny it, but there was no point—my brother knew me.

"It's just that I'm not used to niggas getting the drop on me, and I'm wondering if I'm *slipping*," I confessed.

"Slipping? Because you didn't anticipate that nigga being in bed with a government employee and having his house wired like a bank? Come on, my nigga. How the fuck could you anticipate that when neither Kyndra nor Tink had any idea what was going on?"

He made a logical point, but as a leader, I felt like I was supposed to see through walls and around corners. I didn't have a God complex; I just trusted my instincts. And I felt like I should've tapped into them the moment I put together who Kyndra's dad was. I still might not have anticipated everything that unfolded, but I would've moved with more caution and less emotion. I didn't know how to explain that to Jayson, so I let it go.

"Roll up," I said.

"Oh yeah? Since when do we smoke before a job?"

"This ain't a job because it ain't business. It's *personal*."

He stared at me for a few seconds, then pulled out the gold cigarette case he kept his pre-rolled blunts in. He lit one and passed it to me before lighting one for himself.

We smoked in silence, both of us contemplating what was coming next, even though nothing about it made us nervous. Dropping bodies was an inevitable part of the robbery game because the only *good* witness was a dead one. I wasn't the type to take pleasure in killing usually—it was just business. But the thought of killing my father-in-law had me higher than the watermelon lemonade kush floating through my system.

I was halfway through my blunt when Jayson's phone rang, and I knew by the old-school DMX ringtone it was Blaze.

"Yo," Jayson answered.

He listened for a few seconds, then hung up.

"The Jamaicans are underground planting explosives, but Blaze said it looks like Big Hands is about to leave the house."

"Fuck," I said, putting out my blunt as I stood.

"What you wanna do?"

"We moving on that nigga *now*. Let's go," I said, grabbing the duffel and heading for the door.

"I'ma text Blaze and let him know we're on the move," he said behind me.

I walked outside and headed for the driver's side of the McLaren. Once inside, I passed Jayson the duffel while quickly getting us moving.

"Tell Fabian to control the cameras monitoring the block where this nigga lives, because we're going in hot," I said.

"I'm on it."

As we neared the end of the block, I saw traffic moving at a brisk pace, but I didn't slow down. I power-shifted from third to fifth and jerked the wheel left, mashing the gas. The roar of the V12 drowned out horns as we slid into traffic and shot up the street.

"Try not to kill us before we get there, bruh," Jayson said.

I ignored him and kept pushing the car to seventy mph in under three seconds. We were only ten minutes from Big Hands' block, but I had us fishtailing onto it in under six.

"Where is he?"

"There," Jayson said, pointing to a man walking toward an idling black Cadillac Escalade.

I slammed the brakes, sliding to a stop, snatched the AR-15 from Jayson, then hopped out. Without hesitation I raised it, flipped the safety off, and let bullets fly like confetti on *new years*.

I caught Big Hands in the leg, dropping him, but before I could advance, he scrambled into the backseat. The driver immediately spun a U-turn and sped off.

"Fuck!" I yelled, jumping back into the car.

"You're really 'bout to do this in broad daylight?"

"Shut up and *shoot*," I said, shoving the AR into his hands.

Within seconds I had the SUV back in my sights. Whoever was driving kept weaving so Jayson couldn't get a clear shot.

"Switch to the grenade launcher."

"In the middle of Manhattan? Nigga, are you *trying* to go to jail?"

He wasn't wrong. It was a miracle cops weren't already on us. But we couldn't lose this chance.

"Hold on to something."

Before he could respond, I rammed the Escalade. The back end wobbled, but they kept control.

"You do realize that Escalade is bigger than us, right?"

"The bigger they are, the harder they fall."

I was about to ram them again when the back hatch popped open—and suddenly I was staring into the rotating barrels of a 60mm machine gun.

"What the fuck..." Jayson muttered.

I swerved left, sideswiping a cab. The bullets tore through the front passenger side of the McLaren. I slammed the brakes to keep Jayson from getting shredded. A cab rear-ended us hard.

The Escalade sped off, and I knew I had a decision to make. Instead of chasing, I gambled that I knew the route they'd take.

"If he's running, then you can bet he ain't staying in New York. He'll head for Jersey. I'ma cut him off at the bridge."

Two red lights, a school bus, and a crowd of old people later, I fishtailed onto a street where I could intercept him.

"Get the grenade launcher out."

He shook his head but didn't argue this time.

"I hope you know what the fuck you're doing, bruh."

"You just make sure you don't miss."

I slammed the car to a stop, jumped out with the launcher. Seconds later I saw the Escalade barreling toward us. I raised the launcher, locked eyes with the driver, and fired two grenades through the passenger side window.

The explosion was deafening. The ground shook. Flames shot upward.

But sirens were already close.

"Kwan, let's *go!*" Jayson yelled.

The SUV crashed into a parked delivery van twenty feet away. Perfect sitting target—if I had more time. I didn't.

I ran back to the car and got in. Jayson grabbed the launcher so I could whip a 180-degree turn that left smoke everywhere.

"You're fucking insane, you know that?"

"I'm aware. What's your point?" I said, smiling.

He shook his head.

I hadn't realized how bad I wanted that nigga dead until I got the chance. Reckless? Yes. But I didn't care.

"Make sure Fabian erases *all* footage of our little adventure."

"Already ahead of you. Once I knew you were going all out, I texted him to delete shit in real time."

"What would I do without you, bruh?"

"Mannn, *fuck* you," he muttered.

Fifteen minutes later we were home. Jayson already had disposal for the car arranged and our flight booked.

"Don't tell Tink we're coming. I wanna surprise Kyndra," I said.

"I gotchu. After the stunt you just pulled, though, you might wanna surprise her with a gift."

"You're right. Nothing says 'I killed your pops' like diamonds."

I expected him to laugh, but he was staring at his phone.

"You gotta be fucking kidding me."

"What?"

"This nigga just won't *die*," he said, turning his phone toward me.

At first I didn't get it—then I saw paramedics strapping this nigga onto a gurney. Live footage. Courtesy of Fabian.

Not enough time to double back.

Only one option left.

"It ain't over. We'll just have to kill him at the hospital," I said coldly.

Chapter 8

Kyndra

We touched down at the airport in Jersey a little after 5 p.m., which meant we'd made the trip from Morocco in great time. A rented pearl-white Bugatti was waiting on us as soon as we descended the steps from the plane onto the tarmac, along with a few customs officials. Tink and I flashed our Real IDs, hopped in the car, and took off.

"Do you know exactly where Uncle Kenny would've stashed the recorded video?" Tink asked.

"He's got three different safes, so we're gonna split up and hit them all," I replied, quickly shifting gears while merging onto the highway.

"Where are the safes located?"

"One in the master bedroom, one in the home office, and one in the basement where the wine cellar is."

"Okay, I'm texting Skii now to get her working on the combinations."

"Tell her to hurry that *shit* up, and don't tell Fabian, because we're only twenty minutes away and nobody needs to know we're here," I said, pushing the gas pedal further toward the floor.

Once I hit 70 mph, I set the autopilot and pulled out my phone to text my nigga Melly from Brooklyn so he could meet us a few miles from my father's house with the guns I'd requested. Within moments he hit me back to let me know he was on the New Jersey Turnpike headed toward me now.

64

"We got guns," I said.

"Thank God, because this *shit* is crazy enough without us going in there like *shit* is sweet."

"Stop sounding scary, bitch," I said, sucking my teeth.

"Ayo, fuck you," she replied, sticking her middle finger in my face.

I chuckled softly as I took the car off autopilot and pushed us to 90 mph. Fifteen minutes later, we eased to a stop at the rendezvous spot about ten miles from my father's house, and I dropped a pin so Melly would know exactly where we were.

"Good news, bad news. The good news is Skii has the combinations to all three safes, but the bad news is there's a retinal scan required for all of them," Tink said, looking over at me.

Given my father's level of paranoia, I had suspected we might run into something like this. I already had an idea.

"Tell her to hack the safe's security company and override all security measures. That should let us walk in and open the door with nothing more than the combinations."

"I gotchu," she replied, already texting.

A few minutes later, a navy-blue BMW 950i pulled up beside us on the driver's side, and the window eased down. I lowered mine as Melly pushed me a small duffel bag.

"Thanks, my nigga," I said.

"For what?" he replied with a wink before rolling up his window and pulling off.

"Only you could order guns to be dropped off like Uber Eats," Tink said, chuckling.

"Facts."

When I opened the bag, I whistled softly. Melly had given me a nice little care package: two Dracos, two Sig Sauer .45s, four hand grenades, a Glock 27 with a hundred-round drum, and two extra clips apiece for everything. When I passed Tink the bag, I heard her take a deep breath.

"Damn…did he think we were running up in a bank?" she asked.

"I didn't explain what was going on, only that I needed firepower."

"Enough said, I guess."

Once she confirmed everything was loaded, she nodded. I put the car in gear and pulled off.

The closer we got to my father's house, the more butterflies flipped in my stomach, creating the feeling of a wild roller-coaster ride. I'd never felt this way pulling up to the home where I'd lived after losing my mother at sixteen— but I'd also never felt like my father was the *opp*. For years he'd been my only protection, and that sense of security had blinded me to how dangerous he really was. I saw everything clearly now, and as the massive house appeared ahead, I felt more resolved than ever to take my power back.

"You hit the safe in the wine cellar, and I'll hit the other two," I said.

"Am I just looking for the video?"

"No, because that could take too long. Just clear that muthafucka out."

She nodded and began removing everything from the bag again. I knew I'd have to grab a bag from my old room, but that wouldn't take long. I eased to a stop at the front gate, punched in the passcode, and prayed my father hadn't changed it. The gate swung open silently.

Relief hit me.

"We need to be in and out in under ten minutes, so don't waste a moment. If any staff or security question you, play it cool—but if they *flinch*, light their ass up," I instructed.

"You don't think us walking in with heavy firepower visible is gonna invite questions?" she asked skeptically.

"It could, but I'm betting my father has heightened his security, so seeing us strapped shouldn't raise eyebrows. If it does, just say my dad insists you're always armed."

"Okay, that sounds plausible."

When I pulled the car to a stop at the side of the house, she handed me a Draco, a Sig Sauer .45, and two grenades. I tucked the .45 into the waist at the back of my Capri pants and put a grenade in each cargo pocket.

"We go in through the back door," I said, stepping out.

Tink followed me as we walked casually around to the back, around the pool, and onto the patio that led to the sliding glass door. I punched in another code on the panel, and once the green light flashed, I slid the door open.

I nodded to Tink and pointed her toward the basement, while I took the winding staircase near the kitchen up to the second floor. I went straight to my room at the end of the hallway, grabbed two Nike backpacks from my closet, then doubled back toward my father's room.

Inside, I approached the floor-length mirror beside the walk-in closet and pulled the corner until it swung open like a door to reveal the safe. The keypad's usual glow was gone—meaning Skii had succeeded.

I turned the handle and opened the safe.

I hadn't expected to find something labeled *fed killing*, but a hint would've been nice. Instead there were several CDs with only dates on them, a few flash drives, cash, and guns. I threw everything into one backpack, closed the safe, and pushed the mirror shut.

One down.

I slung the full backpack onto my back, grabbed the empty one, and headed downstairs. I dropped the first backpack in the trunk, then hurried back inside where I ran into Tink coming out the back door.

"You good?" I whispered.

"Yeah, I took everything like you said."

"Okay. Go wait in the car while I hit the last safe."

Her frown was adorable.

"I'm right behind you, don't worry. Just hop in the driver's seat so I can jump in and we can get gone fast."

She understood—even if she didn't like it.

I made my way to my father's office, walking past the kitchen and living room like I belonged there. Inside, I headed straight for the hidden floor safe under the desk. I sat in his leather chair and pressed the button under the armrest to reveal it. The keypad was dark—Skii again.

I pulled the door open and filled the second backpack with more guns, cash, flash drives, and a clear plastic bag of diamonds. The last item was a ledger. I prayed it was incriminating. I grabbed his laptop too.

I zipped the bag, closed the safe, and re-concealed it.

Job done.

As soon as my hand touched the office doorknob, I heard voices out in the hallway. I couldn't make out the words—my heartbeat was thundering in my ears.

I had to stay calm.

I glanced at the Draco in my hand. It made me feel *exposed*, not confident.

But it gave me an idea.

I swapped it for one of my father's Glock .45s and zipped the backpack, then shoved it open and dropped the bag out the window into the bushes. I almost followed—but the office door opened.

Big Frost walked in.

When our eyes locked, surprise flashed across his face. My recovery was faster.

"What is it, Frost?" I asked, like I belonged here.

"I didn't—Ms. Kyndra…when did you get home?"

"Not long ago. Why?"

He studied me, and the silence was unsettling. I kept my expression blank.

"I was just asking because I didn't hear you come in. Are you waiting for your father?" he asked.

Something in his tone was *off*. Maybe because I was in my father's office. Maybe something else.

Either way, I had to play it cool.

"Yeah, I wanted to discuss some business stuff with him, but since he's not here I'll just come back later."

"You're more than welcome to wait for him, you know that," he said, smiling at me.

I knew that his smile was meant to be disarming, but it made the hair on the back of my neck stand up.

"It's *okay*, I've got a few errands to run," I replied, walking toward him and the door.

His smile stayed in place, but it wasn't reaching his eyes, and I knew there was a problem.

"By the way, Frost, where is my father?"

"I'm not sure. Have you tried calling him?"

The lie that left his lips was told so smoothly that the average muthafucka would've swallowed it whole. I wasn't the average muthafucka though, and I knew just how unlikely it was that my father's head of security didn't know where he was at all times. The fact that he'd lied to me meant that, at the very least, he knew my father and I weren't good with each other right now, which meant he was trying to stall me.

I raised the pistol in my right hand and fired two shots, hitting him in the face and chest. His big body hit the floor with a solid thud, but I was more worried about the sound of the gun going off because it was sure to draw attention. I wasted no time stepping over his body and quickly leaving the office, but as soon as I rounded the corner, I was looking down the barrel of four guns.

"Easy fellas, you don't wanna accidentally shoot a pregnant woman," I said, tightening my grip on the Glock in my hand.

I'd halfway expected to see some type of hesitation in the men holding the guns, but no one flinched or blinked. It went without saying that if I moved, then they'd air my ass out—whether I was pregnant or not—which left me with very few options. I dropped the pistol to the floor and slowly raised my hands, but that didn't cause them to lower their guns in the slightest.

I was about to ask them what the fuck was going on when they suddenly stepped apart and created a path for my father to limp through.

"You look like *shit*," I said, smiling broadly.

"Courtesy of your husband, but I'll live. Unfortunately for you all," he replied.

"What makes you think that Kwan had anything to do with whatever happened to you? You've got a *lot* of enemies, Father."

"I know that it was him because I saw him fucking shooting at me as he chased me through Manhattan. Go ahead and call him though, and he'll tell you all about it," he replied.

"That's *okay*... I believe you," I said slowly.

"I don't give a fuck if you believe me. I still want you to call your nigga so that he can understand that he forfeited your life by coming for me."

The pure hatred that I saw in his eyes told me just how serious he was, and the idea of calling Kwan became more appealing. I slowly reached into my pocket and pulled my phone out, silently thinking about the pistol still tucked at the small of my back.

"Put it on speaker phone," he demanded.

I obliged without argument or protest, dialing Kwan's number and listening to it ring. On the fourth ring it was abruptly answered.

"Bae, I can't talk right now—"

"Then just listen. You miscalculated by coming at me and using your pregnant wife to finish your job. Shoot her in the leg," my father ordered.

Before a word could be uttered by me or Kwan, I felt the bullet's burning heat, and I fell to the floor in pain. All that could be heard was my father's maniacal laughter.

Chapter 9

Kwan

"Say what? You wanna run down on this nigga and kill him in a crowded ass hospital?" Jayson asked.

"Can you think of a time when he'll be more vulnerable?" I asked, tapping the screen in the dashboard to GPS locate the nearest hospital.

I knew this shit was getting messier by the minute, but it had to be handled before this nigga had a chance to regroup and strategize. Right now we had the advantage, so it was best to press it.

"Tell Blaze to meet us at the hospital because we need boots on the ground. Send the same message to the Jamaicans," I instructed.

"Bruh, this shit is crazy and *sloppy*."

"Yeah, I know, just send the messages," I said, pulling off and focusing on the directions that said we'd arrive at the hospital in four minutes.

I was mentally trying to organize a plan that wouldn't land us all in some upstate New York prison, but nothing was really popping into the front of my mind. When we got to the hospital I drove around the entire building twice before I backed into a visitor parking space.

"You got a plan?" he asked.

"Nah, not really."

"Going in guns blazing will have the Feds, National Guard, and everyone else on our ass before we make it back to the car. Keep that in mind," he said seriously.

I didn't question his analysis or his prediction because I knew that both were accurate. I was trying to see a way around the inevitability that he spoke of. I was also factoring in the very real possibility that there was a cop or two inside the hospital, because there typically was.

"The Jamaicans are here, and Blaze is on his way. What do you wanna do?" Jayson asked.

"Send the Jamaicans in to find out what part of the hospital Big Hands is in, and what room. This is strictly a recon mission."

"Finally, something that makes sense," he mumbled under his breath.

I didn't respond to his smart-ass comment; I just kept mentally working on a solution for the problem I had with this nigga Big Hands still breathing. Somebody was definitely praying for him because that Escalade getting hit with two grenades should've caused it to explode, but somehow he'd made it out alive. His luck couldn't hold up forever though.

"You realize that you hit him in the leg when we first ran down on him, right?" Jayson asked.

"Yeah, I know."

"So then you know that as soon as a nurse or doctor checks him out and finds a gunshot wound, they'll call the cops," he stated.

"I know that's the protocol, but a nigga like Big Hands ain't 'bout to have the cops questioning him. He'll make sure that this is kept quiet," I replied confidently.

"What makes you so sure about that?"

"Because no matter how much of a polished businessman he is, he's still a street nigga at heart, which means his instincts won't allow him to put the cops in his business," I replied.

Jayson didn't say anything in response, but I knew he understood because we would move the same way if the roles were reversed. The sound of my phone chirping broke the silence, and I looked at it to find a message from Blaze.

"Blaze is about ten minutes away," I said.

"We should send him to the hospital because at the very least we know that Big Hands' people don't know what he looks like."

"Makes sense, but let's see what the Jamaicans find out first."

No sooner had I said that, the sound of his phone going off from a text message filled the car.

I watched as he read the text message, and the frown on his face said a lot before he uttered a word.

"What's up, bruh?"

"They're saying that no one was just admitted from a car accident or a gunshot wound," he replied.

"Is it possible that they took him to another hospital?"

"I doubt it because this was the closest one to where we left him," he said, texting a reply to the Jamaicans.

While he did that, I called Fabian.

"Yo?" he answered.

"Aye bruh, they saying that this nigga ain't in the hospital," I replied.

"Hold on. I'ma backtrack from the scene of the accident and track his movements. I'd been following you and Jayson to make sure the cops weren't looking for you."

His logic made sense, but I didn't like not knowing where the fuck this nigga was. I could hear Fabian's fingers flying across his keyboard until that sound was interrupted by an incoming call on my other line.

"Hold on, Fabian," I said, switching to my other line.

I saw that it was Kyndra calling, and I started to ignore her, but I knew that would only make her worry.

"Bae, I can't talk right now—"

Hearing Big Hands' voice froze the rest of my excuse in my throat as my mind raced to figure out *how* the fuck he was calling me from Kyndra's phone. I listened intently, and what I heard turned my blood into polar ice. The last thing that I heard before the line went dead was that nigga's laughter as my wife screamed in pain.

I immediately got back on the line with Fabian.

"Fabian, track Kyndra's phone because wherever she is, that's where that nigga Big Hands is."

"I gotchu, hold on," Fabian replied.

"Wait, what?" Jayson asked, looking at me with a crazed look in his eyes.

"I heard her, bruh... and I heard him give the order to shoot her in the leg."

"That's impossible because her and Tink are on the yacht, and we know he's here. Maybe he cloned her signal when he talked to her, and he's just trying to throw you off your game by making you think he has her," Jayson said.

His explanation made some type of sense, but my gut told me that he couldn't be more wrong.

"Track Tink," I said, nodding toward his phone.

I knew that if Kyndra had come back to the States, then her cousin would've come with her—meaning my baby and my niece or nephew were in danger too.

"Ayo, her phone is in Jersey, and from the looks of it, him and his people hijacked an ambulance, which is why he never made it to the hospital," Fabian said.

"Tap into the security feed at his house in New Jersey, and tell me what you see. Have Skii send out a message telling everyone to converge on that house," I said, starting the car and racing out of the parking lot.

"We're on it," Fabian replied.

"Tink's location is the same as Kyndra's," Jayson said hollowly.

I understood the feelings running through him right now, and that only made me drive faster.

"Try to call her and see what happens," I suggested.

The odds were high that they were together, but we needed to be sure.

He put the phone on speaker and I heard it ring twice before she answered, whispering.

"Jayson?"

"Tink, where are you, bae?"

"Jay, we fucked up and—"

"It's *okay*, it's *okay*, just tell me where you are right now," he said calmly.

"I'm outside my uncle Kenny's house hiding in the car. Kyndra is inside and I heard gunshots, but I don't know what to do," she whispered emotionally.

Jayson and I exchanged a quick look, and I knew that he wanted to tell Tink to get the hell out of there, but neither of us believed in leaving someone behind.

"Okay, tell me what happened, bae," Jayson said.

"We–We came to get the hard copy of the video uncle Kenny had of Kwan shooting the Fed guy. We thought he'd be too busy with you all in New York to even know we'd been here, but he showed up all of a sudden, and Kyndra was still in the house. I don't know what to do, baby, and I'm scared," she confessed, sounding like she was on the verge of tears.

"Don't do anything, sweetheart. Just stay where you are because we're on our way," he replied reassuringly.

"Kwan, you still there?" Fabian asked.

"Yeah, what's up?"

"I've got eyes inside the house. Kyndra is alive, but she's been shot in the left leg and it's bleeding fast," he replied.

Hearing this caused me to mash the gas pedal to the floor and blow through a red light at 110 mph.

"Is everyone on the way?" I asked.

"Yeah, Skii let Blaze and the Jamaicans know, but we've got another problem. This nigga called for a helicopter."

"We can't let him get on that chopper," Jayson said.

"Tell me something that I don't know," I growled through clenched teeth, shifting gears faster.

"Jayson, I think I've got an idea," Tink said.

"What is it?" he asked.

"All he really wants is the load that we jacked from the cartel, so we give it to him. I know we were all against it at first, but this shit ain't worth dying for," she replied.

"It's deeper than that now, and if he gets his hands on that load then there's nothing to stop him from killing you," Jayson said.

"What do you mean that this is deeper than that?" she asked softly.

I saw Jayson look over at me out of my peripheral vision, and I already knew he was thinking about what had just taken place on the streets of Manhattan.

"We were just in a shootout with him, so no amount of money is gonna make him happy. He wants blood," Jayson replied.

"Oh God. Do you think he killed Kyndra?" she asked.

"She's alive, but he shot her in the leg," I said, loud enough for Tink to hear me.

"Bae, do you have a gun?" Jayson asked.

"Yeah… and two grenades."

It wasn't exactly the arsenal that I would've hoped they'd had, but something was better than nothing. Now we just had to figure out how to use this to our advantage because it was obvious that Big Hands didn't know that Tink was out there.

"Yo, Kwan, we've got action on the property," Fabian said.

"What do you mean?" I asked.

"Four SUVs just pulled up at Big Hands' house in Jersey, and a whole *lot* of Chinese dudes just hopped out," Fabian replied.

"Oh shit, it's going down now," Jayson mumbled.

My mind was moving as fast as my car was, and I immediately recognized that this was the only window of opportunity we'd get to distract this nigga.

"Fabian, where exactly is Kyndra located in the house?" I asked.

"Back hallway, right outside of his office," he replied.

When I looked over at Jayson, I could tell by the sick look on his face that he was guessing at what I wanted the next moves to be.

"Tink, do you think that you can get to her?" I asked.

"How? He might shoot me too."

"He's about to have his hands full in a few seconds, so you and Kyndra will be the last thing on his mind," I replied, weaving in and out of traffic.

"Jayson…" she said.

I knew that she was seeking his approval or she wasn't going in, and I wasn't sure how I felt about that right now.

"Pull the car as close to the back of the house as you can, but *not* until you hear some shots or commotion coming from inside," Jayson said.

"Bruh, Kyndra might not be able to make it to the back door or outside with that gunshot wound. Tink needs to go get her," I said.

"I hear you… but I'm not gonna tell her to risk the life of her or our baby. I got love for Kyndra, but I can't do that," he explained calmly.

The instant rage that I felt toward him and Tink was rooted in the fear that I felt trying to overtake me, and it was a struggle not to react to either. All I could really do was drive as fast as I could.

"Fabian, what does it look like?" I asked.

"Big Hands still doesn't know that he's under attack, but he's definitely about to. Kyndra is still in the same spot, trying to stop the blood flowing from her gunshot wound."

"Shoot his address to me," I said, merging onto the bridge that connected New Jersey to New York and pushing the McLaren up to 160 mph.

A few seconds later my phone vibrated in my lap, and I immediately tapped it against the screen in the dashboard in order to sync my GPS. Once it popped up, I saw that we were still ten minutes out, and that made me push our speed to 180 mph.

"Keep your eyes on the situation because we'll be there in a few minutes," I said.

"I'm on it, and the front gate is open," Fabian replied.

"Jayson, I'm in the back of the house," Tink said.

"I told you to wait until—"

He didn't get to finish his sentence before the sounds of gunshots filled the car like it was one of us shooting.

"The curtain just went up, and Big Hands' men are trying to hold off the Triad. Where are you?" Fabian asked.

"Almost there," I said, focusing all my attention on weaving around the slow-moving cars in front of me.

I was driving so fast that I almost missed the left turn that would put me on the road to Big Hands' house, but I locked the brakes and slid until I could make the turn without running us into the woods. When I hit the gas again, the car fishtailed briefly and then shot forward.

"I'm on the property," I said, shooting through the front gate like a running back finding a hole in the defensive line.

"Big Hands is on the second floor, and Kyndra is by herself, but she's not moving," Fabian said.

I could feel my back teeth grinding, and it took all of my self-control not to scream on Jayson and Tink for her not going in. I drove up on the grass headed straight to the back of the house, and when I rounded the corner, I caught sight of a white Bugatti where Tink sat in the driver's seat.

"Get the fuck out of my ride with your bitch ass," I growled, stopping the car and hopping out.

My phone went in my pocket and my gun came out as I advanced toward the house like I was invading a small country. I quickly skated around the pool, but my movements opening the back door were more slowly because I could hear the sound of gunshots not far away. There was nobody in the back hallway except for Kyndra, and I wasted no time getting to her.

"Baby—Baby, I'm here," I said softly, dropping to my knees to scoop her up.

"K-Kwan," she mumbled weakly.

"It's me, and I got you," I said, lifting her into my arms.

She grunted in pain, but she wrapped her arms around my neck tightly.

"I'm—I'm sorry, Kwan. I was just try-trying to—"

"Shhh, baby, it's *okay* and I understand. I'm getting you out of here," I said, heading for the door.

I moved as fast as I could without hurting her, and I managed to make it all the way to the car without getting shot in the back. I gently placed her in the passenger seat that Jayson had vacated before I rushed to hop in the driver's seat.

"K-Kwan, the bushes."

"Huh?" I asked, confused and looking around.

"Grab the bag in the bushes around the corner," she said, pointing toward the other side of the house.

I pulled around the Bugatti and followed her directions, coming to a stop long enough to grab what she wanted, hop back in, and pull off. I assumed Tink and Jayson were behind us, but I didn't look because honestly I didn't give a fuck anymore.

Chapter 10

Kyndra

2 days later…

The aches in my body felt bone-deep even when I didn't move, so I could only imagine the hell that awaited me when I had to get up from my prone position. For now I was content to just lay here—wherever *here* was—with my eyes closed and my mind refreshingly quiet. I'd been in and out of consciousness enough to know that Kwan had somehow managed to save my life by getting me away from my father, and then a doctor had done the rest by treating my wounds. Getting shot hurt like a *muthafucka*, but my pride was wounded more because my master plan had failed miserably. I'd almost got myself and my baby killed, along with Tink and the baby she was carrying. I knew that I was gonna hear it from both Kwan and Jayson, which was all the more reason for me to keep laying right where I was, resting my eyes.

I focused on my other senses in hopes *of* pinpointing my approximate location, but there was nothing to give it away. The lack of multiple machines beeping, whispered conversations, and the stench of combined sickness with death eliminated the odds of me being in a hospital. I was conscious enough to feel the IV needle in my arm though. The sudden sound of a door opening to my right focused my attention in that direction, and the familiar smells forced my eyes open because I now knew exactly where I was.

"H-How many days has it been?" I asked, trying to clear my scratchy throat and gauge Kwan's mood at the same time.

"Only a couple. How are you feeling?"

"Like I'm in trouble," I replied honestly.

He stared at me blankly for a moment before he crossed the room and sat on the bed beside me.

"In trouble? Why? Because you did some dumb shit that endangered you and our child?"

"Kwan, I was just—"

"Stop. I know what you were doing... and I get it. I don't like it, but I get it," he said, taking my hand in his.

The surge of relief that I felt was powerful enough to be orgasmic, although it was short-lived because I could see that there was still a weight on his shoulders.

"What is it, bae? What's wrong?"

"For starters, your bitch-ass father has more lives than a Siamese cat, and he managed to get away from the Triad. Then there's the fact that I'm wanted by the ATF for lighting up half of Manhattan chasing him," he replied.

"That explains why we're back in Greece where you can't be extradited from. But there's obviously more going on—I can see it in your eyes," I said, squeezing his hand gently.

Despite us being together a short amount of time, I felt like I knew my man, and right now I knew that he was holding something back from me.

"I felt like I was losing my mind once I knew that your father had you and that you were hurt. I was trying to do everything in my power to get to you—to save you and our baby..."

"And you *did*, bae. You saved us both, so why are you beating yourself up about it?" I asked, feeling confused.

"It's just... Well, before Jayson and I got there, we were able to get in touch with Tink because she was outside hiding in the car that you rented. I tried to get her to go in and get you once the Triad had your dad distracted, but she wouldn't move without Jayson's approval, and that nigga told her to stay in the car."

I could hear the anger in his voice, but overlapping it was pain—and the math was quickly done for me. He felt betrayed.

"Where are Jayson and Tink now?" I asked.

"I don't know, and I honestly don't give a fuck. My only concern was keeping you and our baby safe."

"I get that, babe… but he's your brother," I said.

"You're right—he's my brother who left my wife and unborn child for dead. Literally," he replied, with obvious bitterness and anger.

I wanted to argue on Jayson and Tink's behalf, but the longer I thought about it, the more I was able to see my husband's point. Tink and I had been in the game together since we were old enough to understand the shit that my big brothers were into. We'd ALWAYS had each other's back, and it had been *both* of us who came up with the plan to move on my father while he was focused on Kwan and Jayson. I understood that she was pregnant, but that bitch should've come in guns hot because that's what I would've done for her.

"I see the smoke coming from your ears, so I know that you know what I'm feeling right now," he said.

"I do, but I don't know what we do about it now because what's done is done."

"What we do about it is make sure that shit don't happen again," he stated boldly.

"So what are you saying, Kwan? We break up our crews?" I asked, already imagining the fallout—and the new possibilities.

"I'm saying ain't no crew if it ain't no loyalty and trust. That shit is already broke, and I ain't trying to fix a *muthafuckin* thing."

"Okay, so then what? What do we do next?" I asked.

"That don't even matter. All that matters is that we do it together and with people we know that we can trust."

I couldn't deny how much sense his words were making, but I also knew that fighting two wars at the same time was a recipe for disaster.

"Baby, I'm with you—but now ain't the time to make more enemies," I said.

"So what you saying? We supposed to act like shit is all love?" he asked, screwing his face up with a look of distaste.

"I'm saying that you know like I do that every closed eye ain't sleep. My father is the real threat right now, so that's what we need to focus on. In the meantime, we move in silence when it comes to separating our interests from those of the people we can't trust. Let's be smart about this—not emotional."

He stared at me hard for a few moments, but I could see the respect and love that he had for me in his eyes, and I knew that he could see the same in mine. We'd spent our lives in the same role, just on different chessboards, which made our combined potential limitless.

"I've got a few friends in Abu Dhabi, so we can disappear for a while until shit calms down," he said.

"That sounds like a plan. First we need to move the gold and platinum because Tink and Jayson know that it's buried here."

"They knew that it *was* buried here," he said, smiling mischievously.

"And what exactly have you been up to while I was laid up recuperating?" I asked.

"A little of this and a little of that. Suffice it to say that all I was worried about was our future."

"Oh, that sounds wondrously mysterious—and vague as fuck," I replied, laughing.

"Well, you know me."

"I do… now give me the details," I insisted.

"I love it when you're pushy," he said, leaning down to kiss me.

I'd expected a simple peck on the lips, but he put the magic of his mouth to good use, and if I would've had panties on them bitches would've dissolved instantly. When he tried to pull back, I grabbed a fistful of his shirt and made him hold still while I used my tongue in his mouth to make my presence known and felt.

"I know that you know I'm naked under this blanket, and a gunshot wound won't stop me from taking good dick, but I will *not* be distracted," I said, pushing him away gently.

The fire in his eyes looked like the lights at Rockefeller Center during Christmas, and I was yearning to dance within those flames. That was exactly how my ass got pregnant in the first place.

"Okay, um, what were we talking about?"

"Our nest egg for the future," I replied, smiling at him.

"Right. So I had everything loaded into three shipping containers to be sailed to a Freeport in Germany. Once there, the platinum and gold were put into about twenty different crates, and everything is now stored at the Freeport where only you or I can access it."

"You've been busy in the last two days," I said, nodding approvingly.

"Only with the things that I could handle from here because I wasn't about to leave your side. I even got you a nurse, and her name is Macy."

"Ah, so it wasn't you who put this IV in my arm and pumped me full of good dope," I said, giggling.

"Nah, but I watched like a hawk to make sure she didn't give you anything that would hurt the baby."

"He didn't just watch; he made me explain *everything* to him," Macy said, coming into the room.

I'd never met her before, but her sky-blue scrubs and name tag were a dead giveaway. I did a quick appraisal of her golden skin tone, athletic body, and beautiful face that spoke to her Mediterranean heritage, but I didn't feel threatened by her. Shit—the thought of a threesome flashed through my mind, and I felt my cheeks heat up from the blush I felt.

"I'm sorry, I know that he can be a handful," I said.

"Shit, for what he's paying me, I'm not complaining at all," she replied, smiling as she approached the bed from the opposite side.

"You're worth every penny. She's a certified nurse and a doula too," he said, smiling at me.

"Thinking long-term, are you?" I asked rhetorically.

"How are you feeling today, Mrs.—"

"Let me stop you right there because I ain't old enough for you to call me *Mrs.* anything. I'm Kyndra."

"Okay, and just call me Macy. The first thing that I want you to know is that your baby is absolutely fine. I treated your gunshot wound and used a laser to close it, so your leg is fully functional even though you may be experiencing some phantom pains."

"How long before I can ride again?" I asked, looking seductively at my man.

"I don't recommend traveling by horseback anytime in the next week, but you can ride dick anytime you want," she replied nonchalantly.

"Good to know," I said, winking at Kwan.

"Well then, I'll just check you out real quick and I'll let you get to it," she said, giggling.

"It's okay for you to watch," I said, turning my hazel eyes to her sea-blue ones.

"Hmm. Understood," she replied, giving me a knowing smile.

"Naughty," Kwan whispered, chuckling.

"You like it," I said, still staring at Macy.

"Before I say something that'll get me in trouble, why don't I leave you two to get better acquainted, and I'll go handle some business," he said, kissing the back of my hand before standing up.

"Will you make me something to eat, bae?" I asked, gazing at him with a sexy pout.

"You keep looking at me like that and I'ma get you pregnant while you're pregnant," he said, leaving the room.

"Oh damn," Macy said, bursting into laughter.

"Don't encourage him, he's terrible enough," I said, turning my attention back to her.

"He's not so bad... but I'm assuming that you know that since you married him."

"And just how long have you known Kwan?" I asked, very curious about her familiarity.

"Um, since I was about twenty-one, I guess, so that would be five years now. It's not every day you meet a civilized, rich American who doesn't wanna rape and pillage the culture here or use this place as a playground. Kwan has always shown appreciation for Santorini, even supporting the local businesses here instead of outsourcing his wants and needs like most Americans. He's just a good guy."

"That he is, that he is," I said, studying her as she checked the readings on the diagnostic machine I was hooked up to.

"And to answer the questions that you haven't asked: no, I haven't fucked him, and yes, I would *love* to," she stated, looking me directly in the eyes.

"I can respect your honesty."

"Good, because I mean it when I say that I'm not a homewrecker or a whore. What's in between my thighs is a privilege that very few have known, and one of the things that I've always respected about Kwan is that he never tried to talk me out of it. Maybe that made him even more sexy," she said, with a half-smile.

"Where did you two meet?" I asked, more than curious now.

"At the hospital... when he bought it. How did you two meet?"

"In a jewelry store actually… and he bought me this," I said, holding up my hand for her to see my ring.

"Without even knowing you? Yeah, that sounds like Kwan."

"What sounds like me?" he asked, coming back into the room holding a plate in his hand.

"Nothing, just girl talk. There's no way you cooked me an omelet that fast," I said, astonished to see one.

The delicious smells had my nostrils flaring wildly.

"I swear that he's been cooking nonstop for two days, keeping certain things warm and donating others to local shelters and *churches*. He made omelets this morning because he said—and I quote—'that you would wake up today and be hungry.'"

I would've thought that Macy was lying except for the fact that I was looking at the omelet, and now that she'd mentioned it, I could smell food all around me.

"Cooking eases my stress," he said, sitting back down on the bed next to me and cutting up my food for me.

I didn't have to ask if he'd feed me; I just had to lay there and open my mouth. The way that he watched me chew slowly made my pussy throb like strobe lights at a rave.

"Damn that's sexy," Macy said, shaking her head as she quickly left the room.

"Okay, I got a serious question," I mumbled around the mouthful of food I was chewing.

"No, my love, I've never slept with Macy."

"I know that, but I'm curious as to why you didn't?" I asked seriously.

"I don't know. It just never made sense."

To anyone else his answer might've sounded lame, but I knew my nigga so I understood exactly what he was saying.

"How soon do we leave for Abu Dhabi?" I asked.

The way that his eyes immediately shifted downward to the omelet that he was feeding me signaled the bad news before he spoke it.

"I'm flying you to Abu Dhabi tonight… but I've got a line on where your father might be hiding," he said.

"Okay, and is there some particular reason you can't pass that information along to the Triad so that they can do their thing?"

"Because it's personal," he replied simply.

"For *fucks* sake, Kwan, this ain't the time for a dick-swinging contest with my father. Yours is bigger, end of story," I said, trying to control my flaring temper.

"I hear you, baby, I really do… but I've gotta see him die. I don't care *how* he dies or who kills him, but I need to see his heart stop beating."

"Why? What is it that you're not telling me?" I asked, sensing that pieces of the story were missing.

The sudden pain that I saw in his eyes made even less sense than his one-army vendetta, but I was determined to wait on an explanation.

"I've done some horrible things in my life, Kyndra… but it's because of your father that I've done the unforgivable."

"What does that even mean?" I asked, feeling completely lost.

"You know that I did some business with your father years ago…"

"Okay, and?" I asked, after his sentence seemingly got stuck in his throat.

"It was supposed to be a home invasion at first—just a quick break-in and snatch the valuables. Your father had heard from a friend of a friend that I was an up-and-comer who knew his way around houses, and I wasn't picky about eliminating witnesses. So, he found me and offered me the job… only he changed it up a couple days before it was supposed to go down. Instead of just emptying out the house, he wanted me to kill the owner. A woman."

I could tell by the look on his face that Kwan was neither proud nor comfortable with what he'd done, but I still felt like there was something that I wasn't seeing.

"Babe, I know that you did some bad shit before, and so have I. That doesn't make me love you any less," I said sincerely.

"I know that you mean that, sweetheart, but I need you to wait until I've told you the rest."

I felt a familiar rumble in my stomach, like the sound of thunder crackling as you gaze at the storm clouds in the distance. Old folks used to say that they could smell rain coming, and right now I knew exactly what that meant. I was too nervous to say anything, so all I could do was wait on him.

"Your father didn't just want me to kill this woman—he wanted me to do it in a way that wouldn't look suspicious. He told me to make it look like a *suicide*."

I felt my mouth go dry even as it hung open to my chest. The sound of my heart hammering against my lungs was loud enough to make me believe that there was a drummer live and in concert in the bedroom with us. I thought my world had fallen apart when I'd stopped being my daddy's little girl and I became expendable to him. This was worse though.

"S-Suicide? That means you—you killed my mom? It was you... and my dad ordered it?"

Chapter 11

Kwan

The pain in her eyes tore my soul in two like nothing ever had, not even the *loss* of my first child by Rashawna. I'd known that I was gonna hurt her by exposing the truth, but it was better for it to come from me now than for it to be used against me later.

"I didn't know that she was your mother, or your father's mistress. I didn't even know about you, and I thought that your father only had two sons."

"So when exactly did you find out the truth?" she asked, angrily swiping at the tears staining her cheeks.

"I only found out while you were unconscious. I don't know if you remember, but you took a few different flash drives and a laptop from your father's place. One of the flash drives contained the footage from your mom's house, capturing everything I'd done, so I had Fabian do a deep dive into her life. *That's* when I discovered who she was to you, and why he'd had her killed."

"Why? Why did he have my mother killed?" she asked softly.

"Because your mother had gathered evidence of your father's illegal business dealings, along with evidence that he'd orchestrated the plan for your brothers to pull that armored truck job. She was planning to turn everything over to the Feds in exchange for your brothers' freedom, but your dad found out first," I explained.

The look in her eyes kept shifting from pain and anguish to rage, blinking like a traffic light after 2 a.m. in a small town. I wanted to pull her towards me and hold her, begging her forgiveness, but I wasn't about to make this about me. This revelation was deeper than us.

"I can't believe that he would do that, that he could be so heartless... but it all makes sense now."

"What do you mean?" I asked.

"When I spoke to him while I was still on the yacht, he made a couple slick comments about me committing *suicide*, and about me not knowing who you really are. At the time I thought that it was his lame attempt at trying to divide us by causing me to doubt you—and my sanity. Now I know that he was just setting the stage."

I could feel my back teeth grinding as I fought to suppress the fury building inside me as a result of her father's callous disregard for the woman I loved. He'd been intentionally tormenting her, goading her with the nightmares of her past in hopes of completely destroying any hope she had for a peaceful future. If for no other reason than that, he needed killing in the worst way.

"No matter how much you love me, I know that these truths will irrevocably change things between us. I wish they wouldn't, but being realistic is the only way that either of us can face the uncertain future. For now I would imagine that you need to process this without me, and while you do that I'ma go wipe your father's existence from the face of this earth. After that we'll figure out the future, *okay*?"

The glassy look in her eyes told me that she was moving further away from me, but she still managed to nod in answer to my question. I leaned in to kiss her softly on the forehead, then I got up and walked out of the room.

I found Macy in the kitchen sitting at the counter, and I passed her the plate in my hand.

"Get rid of this."

"You okay?" she asked, taking the plate from my hand and putting it in the sink.

"No, because I swore that I'd never hurt her."

"It would've hurt her more if you didn't tell her, and it would've damaged you both long-term," she said.

I'd confided in Macy while still waiting on Kyndra to fully regain consciousness because I'd needed someone who would give me 100% truth, no matter how ugly it was. I knew she was still speaking the truth now, but that didn't erase the image of Kyndra's world being shattered—a picture I would now carry with me forever. Nothing would erase that from my mind.

"I need you to look after her for a while," I said.

"Here, or do you want us to go somewhere else?"

"Stay here for now, but you might have to go to Abu Dhabi on short notice," I replied.

"And where are you going?"

"I'm going to kill a nigga that needs killing," I said, leaving the kitchen and heading for the home office I'd set up.

I wasn't relishing the thought of leaving Kyndra alone, but I knew her father's death would give her more comfort than I could at the moment. When I sat down at my desk, I FaceTimed Fabian to get an update.

"You still in the same place?" he asked as soon as he answered.

"Yeah, why?"

"Because I've got confirmation that ole boy is definitely in Canada. We can meet you there," he suggested.

"Just you and Blaze. Jayson has his hands full with Tink, and I don't want him around me distracted. What part of Canada?" I asked, already making the necessary charter plane arrangements online.

"He's in Québec."

"Okay. You two drive up and cross through Vermont so that you can bring heavy artillery. Bribe whoever you need to in order to make it through customs, and I'll call you when I land," I said, hanging up without needing an answer.

Once I had my flight scheduled, I contemplated whether or not to involve the Triad, but ultimately this hit too close to home now to outsource the job. Big Hands hadn't just ruined his daughter's life—he'd fucked me over and was planning to put my black ass under the penological system at some point. He'd had two flash drives with proof of me doing his dirty work for him, and even the dumbest criminals knew that a murder charge came without a *statute* of limitations. So the bottom line was that Big Hands had tried to kill me—*planned* to kill me—long before I'd made a move against him. There would be no remorse from me for whatever happened next, nor would there be any type of mercy.

After I'd made all the necessary arrangements and calls, I grabbed an overnight bag and tossed a few things inside that I'd need. I knew that I was wanted in New York City, but Canada didn't extradite to the U.S. for capital offenses, so I was still able to travel under my Real ID. I was headed for the door when Macy popped up and stood in my way.

"She wants to see you."

"Just tell her that I'm already gone," I said, attempting to move around her.

"I'm not lying for you, Kwan. Besides, she *needs* to see you," she replied, crossing her arms over her chest and blocking my way.

I knew I could lift Macy's 5'3", 130 pounds out of my way, but in the end I'd feel like a coward for just leaving my wife.

"Put this in the truck for me," I said, passing her my bag and taking a deep breath.

"Gladly. Now go."

"I'm going, I'm going," I said, heading back toward the bedroom Kyndra was in.

I rounded the corner prepared for the tumultuous emotions that had to be causing havoc inside her, but the look on her face was stone cold and emotionless.

"Bae..." I said slowly, unsure what exactly she was thinking.

"I forgive you, Kwan. I know that if you'd known then what you know now you wouldn't have done what you did. So I forgive you."

"Okay..." I replied, sensing that there was more.

"He dies here."

"Come again?" I asked, confused.

"I said, *he-dies-here*. There's no way that you're gonna let me go wherever it is that he's hiding, and I understand because I don't wanna put our baby at risk. But I wanna see him die. I was the one who found my mom—the one who... who had to see her hanging from the support beam in the living room—and I need to see him just as dead. I need you to give me that, Kwan. Please."

I could feel the emotion in her voice, despite how desperately she was clinging to her self-control, and I heard the truth in her words. This was something she truly felt she needed.

"Bae, I can't promise that it'll go down like that," I said.

"Yes you can. You got him here once, so you can do it again. For me."

We both knew she was right, but my concern was that she was asking to ring a bell that couldn't be unrung once he was dead and gone. Her father's life would end, and her nightmares would begin.

"Are you absolutely sure that this is what you want?" I asked calmly.

"Yes, it is."

I stared into her eyes for a few moments, and once I saw that she was completely uncompromising in the matter, I nodded before turning to leave.

I walked outside and climbed into the wheel of my green Range Rover Sport, pulling off while calling Fabian back.

"You on your way?" he asked.

"Yeah, but we're changing the plan. We need to bring him back here."

"You sure about that?" he asked skeptically.

"It wasn't my idea."

He nodded and didn't ask any more questions.

"Ask him how the baby is," a female voice said.

"Who is that?" I asked quickly.

"It's—it's just Skii. We've kinda been—"

"Not my business, but don't let her get you sidetracked," I warned.

"I'm not gonna get him sidetracked, I'm helping with the mission," Skii said defensively, sticking her face in the frame so that I could see her.

"I said what I said. The baby is fine, by the way."

"That's good to know. Do you think that I should call her?" Skii asked.

I contemplated her question for a moment because my initial reaction was to isolate Kyndra so she could deal with her emotions. Maybe it would help to have someone with her that was like family.

"I'll do you one better—why don't you hop the next flight out here and keep her company until we get back," I replied.

"Is this your attempt to keep me away from Fabian? Because I'll tell you right now that he's already pussy whipped," Skii said, laughing.

"What the fuck ever, I'm damn sure not," Fabian replied defensively.

"*Please!* This man fucked me like he ain't had no pussy in at least five good years, and had me damn near walking sideways. Ever since then he ain't let me out of his sight," she bragged, squeezing his cheeks.

All I could do was shake my head, but I didn't say shit because I knew better than most what good pussy could do to a mere mortal.

"*Okay*, well he's gonna have to miss the pussy for a little while, so hop on the next flight," I demanded.

"Yes boss," she replied sassily.

"Bruh, I'm not whipped," Fabian protested.

"It don't matter, my nigga, just focus on a clean extraction. I don't need no witnesses unless they're dead ones. Understand?" I asked.

"I gotchu. Call me when you land," he said, disconnecting the call.

I sent Macy a quick text letting her know that Kyndra had a surprise guest coming, but she wasn't to tell her. I arrived at the airport just in time to see my rented G IV being wheeled out of the hangar and prepped for takeoff. I parked in the hangar, grabbed my bag, and headed toward the plane.

"Good afternoon, I'll be your pilot, and—"

"I don't do small talk, so just get us in the air *asap*," I said, walking right past him and climbing the steps to the plane.

I got comfortable in the first leather chair that I came to, and without asking, a slim, attractive blonde female approached me with a drink in her hand.

"Hi, I'm Kat, and I'll be providing all of your in-flight needs."

Her voice was pure honey fresh off the comb, dripping with a sensuality that could bend a man's iron will. No doubt she was used to playing Burger King when it came to her customers, but I wasn't on that type of time.

"Another Hennessy White and I'll be good," I said, quickly draining the glass and passing it back to her.

She disappeared behind me, and by the time she came back the sounds of the engines powering up drowned out everything else. I accepted the drink from her and leaned back to rest up before I dropped into Canada. My mind was on inflicting as much pain as I possibly could on my father-in-law, but about half an hour after we reached our cruising altitude, I got a phone call that demanded all of my attention. I knew this call would eventually come, but this was sooner than expected.

"And to what do I owe this pleasure?" I asked, answering the phone.

"JaKwan, don't fucking play with me because you already know why the fuck I'm calling," Rashawna said, sounding sexy and *pissed*.

"You know, being this grumpy can have a negative effect on your ovaries."

"I wish you were standing in front of me because I'd punch your stupid ass in the face until you looked like a ruptured ovary!" she yelled.

It was obvious that taking the lighthearted approach wasn't gonna work, so it was time to switch tactics.

"Shawna, will you *please* calm down and let me explain."

"How do you explain this, Kwan? You just did some reckless ass shit that plastered your name to the top of the ATF most-wanted list. I mean, you shot up the *one* city in New York that's populated by most of the wealthiest one-percenters, and the ripples of that shit hit D.C. like a tsunami. What the fuck were you thinking?"

"I was thinking that a muthafucka needed killing by any means necessary, and I was right," I replied, nonplussed by her reaction.

"Nigga, I know you, and you move quieter than this. You move more careful than this, so *please* tell me what the fuck is going on because I'm about a hot second from finding your little wife and asking her in a not-so-nice way."

Her threat wiped the smirk off my face because I knew without a doubt that Shawna was the type of crazy to do some shit like that. Kyndra had enough to deal with, and I wasn't about to invite more drama into her life.

"Yo, chill. I hear what you're saying, and you're right that under normal circumstances I wouldn't have been that loud, but it couldn't be avoided," I said.

"Take it from the top, Kwan, and tell me who the fuck you were shooting at."

"My father-in-law," I replied.

"Oh *wooowww*, this shit is really messy," she said, chuckling humorlessly.

"Tell me about it."

"*Okay*, so why exactly did you have to chase the nigga all over the city?" she asked, sounding a little calmer.

"It wasn't the original plan, trust me. Shit just went bad quickly, and I reacted to it."

"No. You reacted with emotion, and that's something that you just don't do, which tells me that your wife's father did something *serious* to provoke you. That also tells me that whether you're wanted or not, you mean to see this through," she said softly.

"I don't have a choice for real. I grabbed a tiger by the tail, and now my only option is to skin that bastard and make him a throw rug."

"It's gonna be hard to do that with the law looking for you, so *please* tell me that you've got a plan," she said, sighing wearily.

"Yeah, I've got a plan, and don't worry because where I'm going hunting the cops won't be looking for me."

"I wouldn't be so sure. Someone has already called in some huge favors in order to have the ATF gunning for you," she said.

"What do you mean?" I asked, sensing that I'd missed something.

"What I mean is that you covered your tracks well enough—or Fabian did—because there's no actual video footage of your face or you shooting. You're a wanted man because of witness testimony, and I think you know who the witness is."

It was on the tip of my tongue to scream that rat bastard's name, but I controlled my temper with the sure knowledge that Big Hands would get what he so righteously deserved.

"I never knew the word of a known criminal carried such weight," I said.

"It does when he's got politicians, cops, and judges in his pocket. Not to mention federal agents. So I hope you've assembled your best team because this ain't no five-on-five pickup game at the Rucker. This the big boy league."

"Well, you know me, I'm suited, booted, and ready to shoot it," I replied, smiling.

"Yeah, whatever, smartass. Where are you right now? Because I need to see you."

"Shawna, now is *not* the time for a booty call."

"Man, fuck what you talking 'bout. I gotta get mine while I still can because if you die on me before I get my baby, I'ma be pissed," she said in her most serious tone.

"Damn, so all I am to you is a sperm donor? Thanks."

"You know that you're way more than that… I still love you, if you want me to be all the way real," she replied.

I hadn't expected her to be so vulnerable, and now that she had, I really didn't know what to say.

"Kwan, you still there?"

"Yeah, I'm here. You just knocked me off balance a little," I confessed.

"Well shit, now you know how I've felt every day of my life since you walked into it."

"How come we've never had this conversation before?" I asked.

"We have, but I guess you weren't listening. Things between us were always supposed to be fun—and they were—but it got real for me somewhere along the way."

Her open declaration made me think back over the years that we'd known each other, and with each memory came more clarity.

"Yeah… I guess it got real for me too," I said softly.

"Good. Because you better *not* THINK about dying on me, negro. Just do what you gotta do, and I'll be ready to jet to wherever you are when the smoke clears," she vowed.

"In that case, give me a few days and I'll see you."

"That's a promise you better keep," she replied, hanging up before I could say anything else.

I smiled as I sipped the rest of my drink and reclined in my seat. Before I knew it, the liquor had its intended effects, and I was peacefully asleep. I probably would've stayed that way all night, but the feeling of someone gently shaking my arm caused me to stir and open my eyes.

"We're about 10 minutes out," Kat said softly.

"*Okay*, thanks."

"Shall I refreshen your drink?" she asked.

I shook my head no as I sat up and called Fabian.

"Where are you?" I asked.

"At the airport waiting on you. I've got customs and security bought and paid for, just let me know what time you're landing."

"We're 10 minutes out. Do you have an exact location on Big Hands?" I asked.

"As of 30 minutes ago he was at a strip club called Tha 6, with three of their baddest girls in the back room doing something strange for some change."

"What's his security like?" I asked.

"Looks like more secret service than two Presidents visiting a foreign country."

This definitely made things more difficult, but Big Hands had created the necessary distraction by being in a strip club. He may have had niggas watching his back, but them same niggas had one eye on all the scattered ass moving around too.

"How many exits?" I asked.

"Two. One at the back of the building which leads to employee parking, and one on the side that leads to the customer parking."

"*Okay*, we'll talk more once I'm on the ground," I said, disconnecting the call.

I used Google to pull up a map of the club as different scenarios played out in my mind. I liked the fact that the club was only a five-minute drive from the airport, which meant that when shit kicked off it wouldn't take long to get out of dodge.

"Kat?"

"Yes, sir?" she replied, appearing from the back of the plane.

"Tell the pilot that we're doing a quick turnaround, so if he needs to refuel, it needs to be done fast."

"Yes, sir," she replied, heading for the cockpit.

With that taken care of, I put my mind back on the kidnapping that was about to go down. The great thing about strip clubs was that there was always a lot going on. The bad thing was that there were sure to be casualties of innocent people, and that wasn't gonna go over nicely with the Canadian Prime Minister. I guess it was a good thing that I wasn't a politician.

By the time we landed and came to a stop, I had an idea of how this was about to happen, and it was definitely gonna be messy.

"Did you bring a grenade launcher?" I asked Blaze, as he met me at the bottom of the plane's steps.

"I try not to leave home without one," he replied, chuckling.

I gave him a pound and then climbed into the back of the gray Cadillac Vistiq idling a few feet from the plane.

"What up, bruh?" Fabian asked, passing me a chrome fully automatic Glock .27 with a hundred-round drum attached to it.

"Same ole shit, just a different country," I replied.

Once Blaze slid behind the wheel, we pulled off into the darkness.

"How do you wanna do this?" Blaze asked.

"How many men do we got?" I replied.

"Twelve, not counting us, already inside throwing a fake bachelor party," Fabian said.

"They got eyes on our man?" I asked.

"Nah, but there's cameras on the back hallway and he ain't came out yet. He's got two niggas posted up outside the door, and everybody else is in the front of the club," Fabian replied.

I let this information roll around in my head, and by the time we reached the club, I knew how I wanted to play it.

"Yo Blaze, you take the back with me. Fabian, you take the side just in case someone tries to slide out that way. Tell them niggas inside to start shooting, and when they do that, Blaze, you knock the back wall down with the grenade launcher."

"Sounds like a straight bum rush," Blaze said, smiling.

"Exactly," I replied.

"When do they start shooting?" Fabian asked.

"Now. Right—the fuck—now," I replied.

Chapter 12

Kyndra

12 hours later

I tried my best to sleep, knowing that my body and my baby needed the rest, but every time I closed my eyes I saw my mother. I didn't see her as the happy, vibrant, gorgeous woman that she'd always been. It was her in her last moments… with her beautiful hazel eyes bulging from their sockets, and her tongue hanging from her open mouth like some possessed beast. My father hadn't just paid to snuff out her life, he'd paid to steal her beauty as well. All these years I'd questioned how she could love me so much but not care enough to walk through life with me until God called her home. Now I knew that she'd had no intention of leaving me prematurely. In fact, she'd been trying to give me everything I wanted and needed by trying to bring my brothers home, and get me from under my father's thumb before it was too late. Knowing that I'd had an amazing mother eased the pain somewhat, but it made the hole in my heart bigger because I missed her that much more.

"You're supposed to be sleeping," Macy said, from the shadows of the doorway.

"And you're not supposed to be hovering."

"Actually I am, because it's part of the job, and I would never let Kwan accuse me of not doing a good job taking care of you," she said, sounding way too serious.

I couldn't see her face in the moonlight, only her form, but her voice was telling her secrets.

"You know who Kwan really is, don't you?" I asked.

"Wh-What do you mean?"

"Answering a question with a question is a great stall tactic, but not one that you need. I believe you when you say that you've never fucked my husband... but I also think that it's more than his looks and charm that make you want to," I replied.

She didn't speak for a few moments, and I was guessing it was because she was trying to figure out how much she should tell me. She moved slowly, bringing herself out of the shadows in her plain black T-shirt as she came and sat beside me.

"Kwan isn't the first man I've met with two sides to him, but he's the first one that I felt safe with," she confessed.

"Yeah, I can understand that feeling... what happened that allowed you to see his *other* side?"

"I had a boyfriend named Mike... and he was a mean drunk. He'd hit me before, but nothing serious, until one day he shattered the orbital bone around my left eye socket. I was too ashamed to tell my parents, let alone the cops, so I came to Kwan for a place to hide and heal. He didn't ask any questions until I was ready to talk, and once he knew the whole truth he never once judged me. Mike called me everyday for a week, leaving me sappy messages of apology one minute and then threatening to kill me if I didn't come back to him. I just couldn't deal with it..."

"And so Kwan did," I said, knowing my husband.

"I never asked him outright, but suddenly the calls and texts from Mike stopped, and Kwan told me that I didn't have to worry about him anymore. To this day they've never found his body, and everyone just thinks that he went off to explore the world."

"Kwan can be very protective of the people that he cares about," I said.

"Sounds like you know this from some experience yourself."

"Are we trading war stories now?" I asked, chuckling softly.

She didn't respond, but I knew she was waiting.

"Let's just say that I've had a front-row seat when it comes to his protective and deadly instincts, and it only made me love him more afterwards," I confessed.

"Bet it made your pussy wet too," she said, chuckling.

"Mmm, you speaking from experience again?"

"Hell yeah!" she admitted, laughing as she laid down beside me.

"You know, if you weren't so obviously emotionally attached to him, I might suggest that the three of us have a little fun in this bed. But I have a feeling that things would get complicated and messy."

"You're probably right… and no one wants things to get messy," she said, reaching beneath my shirt and gently caressing my thigh.

"Wh-What are you doing?" I asked, trying to keep my voice steady.

"Just trying to help you get to sleep."

Her words were whispered right next to my ear, and seconds later I felt her incredibly soft lips on my neck. At first my body tensed, but when her fingers started to gently rub my clit everything in me relaxed. The more she rubbed, the wider my legs spread, until I felt like I'd do the splits if she kept going.

"M-Macy," I panted.

"Shhh," she replied, kissing me with a fiery passion.

I opened my mouth to her and turned my brain off, willingly following her wherever she led. As the heat of our kisses intensified, I felt her fingers leave my clit and slip in between my pussy lips before she used two of them to push inside me. I was so wet that I could feel my juices dripping even as my walls collapsed around her fingers like they were a hard dick. She fingered me gently and set my body into a rhythm that had my hips pushing back at her, but when she added her thumb to rub my clit, my back arched. My moans were trapped within the heat of her sweet tongue as my body quickly heated up with insatiable need. I was seconds away from cumming when she stopped, leaving me in a state of confusion and panic. My mouth was fixed to ask her what she was doing, but as soon as she slid down in between my thighs I knew.

Without thought or request, I placed one of my thighs on each of her shoulders and pulled her head towards my pussy with overwhelming need for complete satisfaction. She sucked on my clit like a Now and Later, and my body was pure putty in her hands.

"H-Holy shit!" I panted, gripping her long hair in hopes that it would keep my world together.

The moment that she started to hum with my clit in her mouth that hope flew out the window, and I came loud enough to wake the neighbors. The climax was so intense and it happened so fast that I was left breathless, my head spinning way up in the clouds.

"Wh-Where did you learn to do that?"

"Women's anatomy was always my favorite subject, and I paid close attention after my first girlfriend turned me out," she replied.

I giggled girlishly, and without shame.

"Are you trying to turn me out?" I asked.

"Un uh, just put you to sleep."

Before I could tell her that I felt a strong nap coming on, she was back face-first in my pussy, sucking my juices like they were bottled by Pepsi. She was still mindful enough to be gentle with the leg that I'd got shot in, and I appreciated that even more when she bent me further in half so that her tongue could dance across my asshole. I felt the air get stuck in my lungs as she licked me like my favorite tabby cat, coaxing my asshole to relax enough for her to snake her tongue inside me that way. I was so lost that all I could do was whimper, but she took no mercy on me still. Every time

I got used to the fast rhythm of her tongue, she'd slow the tempo, which only increased the pleasurable pain of a prolonged orgasm. I lost all sense of time, and after cumming twice I finally lost consciousness and passed out in a sex-induced coma.

I awoke to the sounds of birds chirping outside my bedroom window, and Macy curled up beside me sleeping peacefully. I had no incentive to move, so I closed my eyes again until the sound of someone knocking on the front door interrupted my plans for sleeping in.

"I'll get it," Macy mumbled, climbing from the bed and stumbling out into the hallway.

I was waiting to hear the sound of voices, but instead I heard the unmistakable sound of a shotgun slide being racked. Panic flooded my bloodstream, and it wasn't the sexual variety I'd experienced a few short hours ago. Adrenaline had me swinging my legs to the floor as I carefully pulled the IV from my arm. I expected the pain in my leg to be excruciating, but it was tolerable and I was able to stand up.

"Hey Kyndra, do you know a girl named Skii?" Macy hollered.

"Yeah, that's my sister!" I yelled back.

A few moments later Skii came around the corner, looking clearly annoyed, but her face lit up once she saw me.

"So you gotta get shot for me to see you in person?" she asked, stepping into my open arms.

"God I hope not, because that muthafuckin shit *hurt*," I replied, hugging her tightly.

Macy came around the corner with a Mossberg pump 12-gauge shotgun slung over her shoulder like the fucking woman king.

"Ah, I can see the family resemblance," Macy said sarcastically.

"Uh, sis, is she your bodyguard or your girlfriend?" Skii asked, glancing back at Macy.

"I don't know, a little of both I guess," I replied, laughing at how cute Macy looked when she was jealous.

"Yeah well, I'ma need you to get homegirl straight," Skii said, not cracking a smile.

"Sorry, I ain't straight. I play for both teams," Macy replied, winking before turning and leaving the room.

"Wow. So this is what your life is like now?" Skii asked, sitting on the bed.

"Bitch shut up, and tell me what you're doing here."

"Wellll, my man is with your man, so I figured that I'd come keep you company," she replied.

"Aww, that's sweet of you—wait, hold up—did you *just* refer to Fabian as your MAN?" I asked, nudging her playfully.

"Shut *up*! Don't make it a big thing. I just—we just speak the same language, you know? That type of connection ain't easy to come by."

"I know what you mean," I said, smiling as I thought about Kwan and what he meant to me.

My father had tried to poison our marriage, poison my mind against the one person who probably understood me more than anyone else in the world. Seeing the joy in Skii's eyes only strengthened my resolve to never give this type of love up.

"Even though I've got a new man in my life I've still missed you a lot," she said, hugging me again.

I knew she probably did miss me, but she missed her sister Skylar too, and that knowledge made me feel guilty as fuck.

"I'm sorry that I haven't been around. Shit has been more than crazy."

"I get it, especially with all the drama with your pops," she replied, pulling back and giving me a sympathetic look.

"How much do you know?" I asked, feeling vulnerable.

"Probably more than you at this point, because I know that Kwan is trying to keep your stress levels to a minimum."

"The only thing that will do that is watching my father die slow," I replied sincerely.

"Well, I'm sure that you'll get your wish just as soon as they can snatch him up and smuggle him out of Canada."

"Canada?" I asked, genuinely surprised.

"Yep. It would seem that your father headed further north, and he most likely won't expect Kwan to try and hit him again after what went down in Manhattan."

"And what exactly went down in Manhattan?" I asked, wondering how much of the story my sweet husband didn't tell me.

"Shit, a video is worth a million likes, so look for yourself," she said, pulling her phone out.

Once she'd pulled up the footage she passed me the phone and pressed play. As soon as I saw Kwan hop out the car I could tell that he wanted all the smoke, and my eyes were glued to the screen.

"Damnnnn," I mumbled, in awe of how extreme my nigga had gotten in broad *fucking* daylight.

"That's the same shit I said, and I was watching it in real time. Your husband don't play."

The more I watched the more I saw, and the more I saw the more disbelief I felt.

"This nigga was all in for real though," I said.

"What are you looking at?" Macy asked.

I hadn't even heard her come back into the room, but I angled the phone so that she could see the rest of the video play out.

"Mmph," Macy mumbled.

"Translation please," Skii said.

"Her pussy is wet as a muthafucka," I said, running the video back from the top.

"Well if you get off on all that violence then you're definitely in the right house," Skii said, chuckling humorously.

"What does that mean exactly?" Macy asked.

Skii looked at me and I looked at Macy, trying to decide how much I wanted to tell her.

After what had happened between us last night it seemed kinda crazy to hold back, but good head was a far cry from being an accomplice to murder.

"How much do you really wanna know?" I asked.

"Kyndra, you know where my loyalties lie," she replied.

"I do… so it's only fair to tell you that Kwan is bringing someone here to die," I said.

"Why would he bring someone *here* of all places? I mean, I know how much he loves it here, and that this place has been like a sanctuary, so it doesn't make sense that he'd bring someone here to kill them," she replied.

"It does because he's doing it for me. The man that he's gonna kill is the same man that he's gunning for in that video… that man is my father."

"Ooooh," she said slowly.

"Yeah, kind of a mic-drop moment," Skii said, taking her phone back.

"I just need it to be done and over with so that we can move on with our lives," I said sincerely.

"I hear that," Skii said.

"I'ma hit Kwan up and see what he needs to get the job done," Macy said.

"And why would he tell you that?" Skii asked, looking at her with open suspicion.

"It's okay, Skii, I trust Macy and Kwan."

Macy smiled in triumph as she left the room, but I could feel the heat radiating from the woman sitting next to me.

"You know this bitch wants to fuck your man, right?" Skii asked.

"Ain't nothing wrong with my eyesight or my intuition, so I'm well aware of what she feels and why it'll *never* happen."

"Okay, as long as you know. Now the next topic is this business with your pops. That shit ain't just gonna go away once he's dead, so are you mentally prepared to carry his death with you forever?" she asked.

"To be real with you, that man is already dead to me. He's to blame for me losing so many people that I love, including Skylar, so his death will bring me peace."

Skii took my hand and gave it a gentle squeeze, reminding me of something that her sister had done many times before.

"Okay, so I've never been to Santorini, Greece, and we got some time to kill, so let's get out the house for awhile. I picked up Kwan's Range Rover at the airport."

"You know if you put a scratch on that muthafucka he's gonna have your ass," I said.

"Yeah, yeah, just take a shower and get dressed. I'ma open a window because it smells like pussy in here."

"Yeah, but it's good pussy, bitch," I said, laughing as I moved slowly towards the bathroom.

After pulling off my T-shirt and putting my hair in a ponytail I turned on the hot water and hopped in. The pounding pressure of the water was soothing, but if I was really being honest then I had to admit that Macy's nighttime remedies had done my body great. My leg was still sore, but the hot water helped loosen it up, and by the time I got out of the shower 20 minutes later I was only walking with a slight limp.

Back in the bedroom I found a plain white T-shirt, some blue jean shorts, and a Sig Sauer P229 with an extra clip laid on the bed. I had no doubt that Macy had chosen my clothes and accessories, which made me smile as I quickly got dressed. I stuck the clip in my pocket, tucked the gun in the back of my shorts under my T-shirt, and stepped into my Gucci flip-flops before heading to find Skii.

I was surprised to find her sitting at the kitchen table talking in a civilized manner.

"Be careful, it's the convo that lures you, and the next thing you know she'll be trying to turn that ass out," I warned, going to the fridge for some orange juice.

"I don't know, sis, I might give her a run for her money," Skii said confidently.

"Well one day the three of us will have to get together and, uh, compare notes," Macy replied, smiling wickedly.

"Do I need to bring the baby oil?" I asked, laughing.

"Baby oil? Bitch this ain't no Diddy party," Skii replied, laughing with me.

"Definitely not," Macy chimed in, shaking her head.

"Okay, Skii, where do you wanna go?" I asked, pouring myself a glass of juice and putting the container back.

"Macy was telling me about this restaurant not far from here."

"Macy, you coming with?" I asked.

"Nah, I've got some things to do around the house," she replied, giving me a knowing look.

"Are they—did everything go alright?" I asked, feeling suddenly nervous.

"You know Kwan," Macy said, smiling.

That put me at ease somewhat, allowing me to drink the juice to settle the butterflies in my stomach. I made sure to grab my phone off the counter when I put the empty glass down, and then I turned to Skii.

"Hand over the keys and let's go."

She handed me the key fob with a pout on her face, but I ignored her silent plea and led the way outside to the truck.

"So do you wanna eat first, or do the girl things and get mani-pedies?" I asked.

"It's—uh—it's up to you."

I could hear the unexpected emotion in her voice, and I knew that it came from the sisterly bonding she used to do with Skylar. They would get their feet and nails done while sipping champagne or mimosas, and then eat until they could barely walk. Sometimes Tink and I would go with them, and we'd have a helluva girls day.

"Okay, so look up places for us to get pampered while I drive," I said, climbing behind the wheel.

She followed my lead, and we left the house headed for the restaurant first.

The place that Macy had recommended was quaint, almost like a bistro, and they had developed a reputation for having the best Mediterranean food around. When we got there and got seated outside with our menus, we ran into the problem of not knowing exactly what we wanted to eat because it all looked so delicious. The only solution was for us to order a little bit of everything, with a bottle of red wine.

We ate, we laughed, and drank just like old times, and then we waddled our little fat asses back to the truck. Our next stop was the nail shop. We got our feet done first and then our nails, while limiting ourselves to one glass of champagne apiece because the wine already had us buzzed.

"I sooooo needed this," I said, smiling at her.

"Tell me about it. My feet have been hollering for attention, and now that I got a man who gives me *all* that attention, I gotta make sure I keep my shit sexy."

"Wait, you got the nigga sucking toes already?" I asked, cackling with laughter.

"Shit, after the first time I sucked the skin off his dick he's been down to suck, lick, and eat anything I want him to. This juicy booty included."

"Ohhh, you so nasty, and I *fucking* love it!" I said, giving her a high five with my left hand because my nails were still drying on my right.

"I'm not saying this is gonna lead to marriage, but I can definitely see it being a *Love Jones* thing," she said, blushing.

"Well if it *does* become a marriage thing then I better be your maid of honor."

Tears instantly sprung up in her eyes, but I could tell that they were ones of happiness.

Our tender moment was interrupted by my phone going off, and I only answered it because it was probably Kwan checking in. When I saw the house phone number on my screen I was hopeful that he'd made it back already, and I could feel the familiar butterflies in my stomach.

"Bae, are you home?" I asked, as soon as I answered.

"It's—it's Macy. You need to come home."

"Why? What's wrong?" I asked, immediately picking up on the distress in her voice.

"Nothing's wrong, just come home," she demanded, hanging up in my ear.

"What's going on?" Skii asked.

"I don't know, but she sounded weird and she's insisting that I come home."

I could tell right away that Skii was picking up on my vibe, but she wasn't panicked.

"Well, our nails are done so let's go see what the issue is," she said, standing up.

I followed her lead, paid the nail techs, and headed back outside to the Range Rover.

Once we were on the move I had an idea.

"Check with Fabian and make sure everything is smooth out there."

She pulled her phone out and sent the text, and I slowed my speed a bit to give him more time to respond back. It was a long 15 minutes before we got to the house, and Fabian still hadn't texted back, which had us both feeling all types of nervous.

My mind was so focused on Kwan and what could've gone wrong that I almost missed the fact that there was a silver Aston Martin parked in our driveway.

"Skii, hack into the Ring cam on the house and see who that car belongs to."

"Okay, give me a sec," she said, making her fingers fly across her phone's screen.

In less than 30 seconds she was showing me the last two people to walk in my front door.

"Did you know that Tink and Jayson were coming to town?" she asked.

"I didn't, and Kwan didn't either because he would've warned me."

"You say that like they're the opps or something," she said, looking at me quizzically.

"They might be, I don't know yet. I want you to take my gun and wait here for 10 minutes before you get out, and sneak around the back of the house."

"Are you serious? I mean, it's your cousin and brother-in-law," she reasoned.

"Exactly. The same two people who left my black ass for dead. Literally."

Chapter 13

Kwan

As soon as the first shots rang out you could feel the mood in the air shift. The screams reminiscent of classic horror movies quickly rose in pitch, competing with the automatic gunfire and ensuing stampede.

"Do it," I instructed, standing next to Blaze.

He quickly fired two grenades through the back door that was made of glass, and a few seconds later the ground shook while the strip club opened like a broken piggy bank. I immediately saw that Big Hands' two men in the hallway were stunned, and I took advantage of that by raising my gun and knocking their faces off with hot bullets.

"Go get him," I demanded, not moving from my position as my eyes scanned the parking lot for threats.

Gunshots and screams could still be heard with the quality of HD surround sound, but I didn't hear the sounds of sirens approaching yet. Glancing at my watch, I saw that we were still under a minute, which probably left us about three minutes before the Canadian Mounties showed up. When I looked back towards the club, I saw men in suits with guns out in their hands making their way up the hall toward the room Big Hands was in. I swiftly cut them down like I was mowing grass. A few seconds later Blaze appeared with Big Hands thrown over his shoulder like he was a firefighter, and Fabian was covering their escape from the building. As soon as I saw that they were clear I ran for the driver's side of the Cadillac Vistiq and slid behind the wheel."Let's go, let's go,"

I urged, checking my watch again because now I did hear sirens floating on the night air.

Once everyone was loaded up, I left a cloud of smoke and burned rubber as I peeled out of the parking lot.

"He dead?" I asked.

"Nah, I just gave him a little bump on the head so he'd go to sleep," Blaze replied.

"You should've shot his punk ass," Fabian said.

"Nah, I don't want him bleeding out, and we've still got a long flight ahead of us," I said.

I thought about calling Kyndra to tell her that things had gone according to plan, but I wasn't about to jinx us. I drove slightly above the speed limit which put us back on the airport tarmac inside of three minutes, and I was thankful to see that the plane was ready. As soon as we pulled up Kat poked her head out, and then I saw her yell something to the pilot. Seconds later the engines fired up, and I felt that much closer to freedom. We all hopped out and I let Fabian, Blaze, and the still unconscious Big Hands get on board before climbing the stairs myself.

"Kat, we're gone," I said, flopping back into the same leather chair that I'd previously occupied, while taking a deep breath.

By the time the plane started rolling for takeoff Blaze had Big Hands zip-tied securely, and Fabian was on his MacBook probably erasing our digital footprints.

"That went smoothly," Blaze said, sitting beside me.

"Like taking candy from a baby," Fabian said, smiling.

I didn't say anything, I just kept staring out into the darkness seeing all the pain that this man had caused me without me even knowing it. A part of me felt both dumb and naïve because I'd never let any nigga play me so thoroughly in my life. I was used to pulling the strings, but this nigga had been pulling mine, and that truth left a hollow feeling in my stomach. When Kat approached me with a drink in one hand and the Hennessey bottle in the other I took the bottle, and drank straight from it. She didn't ask any questions or make a comment, she just went and got another bottle to serve Fabian and Blaze with.

"Yo Kwan, what's up?" Blaze asked.

"Ain't nothing," I replied.

"Come on bruh, I been knowing you too long for that, so what's up?" He insisted.

"I'm good bruh... its just a lot going on right now," I said.

"Sweetheart, why don't you excuse us for a minute," Blaze said, relieving Kat of the liquor bottle in her hand.

She nodded and headed to the back of the plane where she disappeared behind a door. Her exit made it obvious to me that Blaze wasn't gonna let shit go, plus I could feel him staring a hole in the side of my head.

"This nigga played me for a sucka," I said, nodding towards the unconscious man on the floor.

"How could you have known that all those years ago bruh? I mean, I know you're smart, but you ain't psychic," Blaze said.

"And you were just getting your feet wet in the game," Fabian added.

"I hear you, but the facts are the facts. That bitch ass nigga played in my face," I said angrily.

I took a long drink from the Henny bottle to try and calm nerves.

"He's gonna get his just as soon as we get to your spot, so don't even worry bout it," Blaze reminded me.

Even though I heard his words that were meant to reassure me, they still felt hollow. I quickly realized that I didn't wanna wait to extract my revenge. I wanted my pound of flesh now."Ayo Kat!" I called out.

Within seconds she poked her cute little head back out the door, waiting for instructions."Bring me a sharp knife real quick," I demanded.

She nodded curtly and retreated back into the room.

"What you need a knife for?" Fabian asked, sounding confused and a little worried.

I ignored the question and took one more hit from the bottle of Henny, and then I sat it down as I stood up. I flipped Big Hands over on his back and I sat straddled across his chest.

"What are you doing?" Blaze asked.

"He played in my face, so I'ma play in his," I replied, smiling.

When Kat came out of the back she had an old school switchblade that looked decently sharp on both edges.

"Yours?" I asked, smirking at her.

"A girl can never be too careful," she replied, giving me a wink as she passed me the knife.

I didn't bother to question what she was into, I just put my focus on the nigga trapped beneath me. I placed the blade to the side of his face and began to slowly drag it along his hairline, giving him a crazy sharp shape up. His blood flowed freely and he immediately returned to the land of consciousness screaming like a straight bitch.

"Shut the fuck up," I growled, digging the knife in deeper.

He bucked wildly beneath me, but I rode his chest like he was a wild stallion that needed breaking."Yo Kwan, chill," Blaze said.

I ignored him and kept right on dragging the knife down the side of his face, and up under his chin. By the time I'd made it completely around his face with the blade his screams were pitching higher than the jet's engines, but everyone inside the plane had gone completely quiet. When I looked around I saw the stunned expressions on Blaze and Fabian's faces, and Kat had disappeared back into the room at the back of the plane.

"Pl-Please, just kill me," Big Hands begged.

"You sound pathetic nigga, so just save your breath. You don't get to die until I say so," I replied, using the knife to dig deeper under the flesh of his hairline.

The sound of his screams continued getting louder, and with each one I could feel the smile on my face spreading wider.

"Kwan, you're gonna kill him like that," Blaze warned.

"Nah, he won't die of blood loss. Not yet anyway," I said confidently.

With the precision and patience of a surgeon I continued to cut and slice the flesh of his face away from his skull until he looked like something straight out of a horror flick. When I had completed my task I held it up to the light like a trophy, and inspected it as if it were a new human discovery.

"I ain't never took a nigga's face off before, but I gotta admit that I did good work," I said proudly.

"Is he-Is he dead?" Fabian asked.

"No, he just passed out from the pain," I replied.

"Yoooo," Blaze mumbled softly.

When I looked at him I was surprised to see that he was damn near pale, and he looked like he was gonna be sick.

"You okay bruh?" I asked.

"Are you?" He countered.

"I gotta say that I do feel better," I said, climbing off Big Hands and reclaiming my seat.

I gently laid his face down beside the bottle of Hennessey, admiring it the way someone might look at a beautiful piece of rare jewelry, or a priceless piece of artwork. The blood that covered my hands reminded me of the way a painter would look when he was hard at work, and I wiped them on my clothes with the same disregard I imagined them using.

"Kat," I called out.

It took her a little longer to poke her head out, but eventually she reemerged and stood in the doorway.

"Your knife," I said, holding it out towards her with the blade still dripping blood and tissue.

"Y-You can keep it," she replied, giving me an uneasy smile.

"Thank you. It'll be a nice souvenir to remember this trip by," I said, closing it and sliding it into my pocket.

I could feel Blaze and Fabian both staring at me, but I ignored them and picked the liquor bottle back up to resume drinking. After awhile I felt the effects of the liquor take ahold once again, and I was able to drift off to sleep. My sleep was dreamless, but peaceful, and I didn't wake up until the plane touched down on the runway. I'd expected to see Fabian and Blaze just waking up too, but they were both in deep conversation sitting across from each other a few feet away."You niggas look too serious," I said, stretching like a large cat.

They both looked at me silently before their eyes fell to the floor. I followed their gaze and saw that someone had put a towel over what was left of Big Hands' face. I chuckled softly as I reached for the bottle of Hennessey and took a quick shot to fully wake me up. The plane taxied into the hangar before coming to a stop, and that's when Kat came back out of the room."Is there-Is there anything else that you need?" She asked, hesitantly.

"Can I count on your discretion?" I asked.

"Yes, absolutely."

I studied her without saying a word, evaluating the fear in her eyes and wondering if it was enough to keep her quiet.

"Fabian, wire her a million dollars," I ordered.

"You don't have to do that," she said quickly.

"I know," I replied.

Fabian summoned her to where his laptop was, and while they got that done I cleaned up by putting Big Hands' face in my pocket before getting up with my gun to exit the plane.

When I reached the bottom of the steps I was surprised that my Range Rover wasn't where I'd left it, and I began mentally running different scenarios that could explain why this was. I knew that nobody had stole my shit, so maybe Kyndra had just sent for it for some reason. I started to call her and ask her about it, but I was still intent on surprising her. The question now was how the fuck was I supposed to transport my surprise to her.

"Hey Kat, come here," I said.

A few seconds later she appeared, coming down the steps hesitantly like she was unsure of my intentions.

"Yeah?"

"I need a ride, preferably an SUV," I replied.

"Okay, give me a minute," she said, hurrying into the offices of the plane charter company.

"We good?" Blaze asked, standing in the doorway at the top of the steps.

"Yeah, but my truck ain't here."

"You think somebody stole it?" He asked.

"I don't think nobody is that stupid," I replied.

"Where did ole girl go?" He asked.

"To get us a ride. You and Fabian get ready to move."

Once he disappeared back inside the plane I pulled my phone out, and tapped into the GPS on my Range Rover to see where it was at. Finding it sitting at my house left me feeling relieved, but confused as to why Kyndra would do that considering that it was her idea for me to bring her father back. I looked up at the sound of an approaching vehicle, and I spotted Kat behind the wheel of a Ford Explorer. She pulled up at angle to the plane, giving easier access to the trunk.

I looked around the dimly lit hangar to make sure there were no nosy people loitering around that I'd have to shoot.

"Ayo, let's move," I called out.

A few seconds later Blaze came out carrying Big Hands and within a few moments everybody was loaded up in the SUV. I debated again whether I should shoot Kat, but in the end I decided to spare her life as I slid behind the steering wheel. I laid my gun in my lap and kept my eyes peeled for cops as I pulled off.

"You want me to track your Range Rover?" Fabian asked.

"Nah, I already checked the GPS and it's at my house."

"Maybe Kyndra had Skii drive it in order to get to your house," Fabian said.

"I didn't even think about that, but it makes sense," I replied.

"Your mind is obviously occupied with other things," Blaze mumbled, under his breath.

"Say what you gotta say my nigga," I said, feeling my building frustration.

"You trippin my nigga, that's what the fuck I'm saying. First the stunt you pulled in New York, and now you taking niggas face like you're Hannibal Lecter. Come on bruh, this nigga got you off your game, and I know you see that," Blaze said.

"Yeah, I see it, but it is what it is at this point. That nigga dies tonight, and then shit goes back to normal."

"I know that you believe that, but I sincerely hope you realize how it puts us all in a fucked-up situation when you crash out like this," Blaze said.

"It sounds like you're questioning whether or not I can still lead this crew," I said.

I made sure to look him in the eyes so that he could feel the heat coming with the accusation.

"This ain't a mutiny, bruh," Fabian said.

"You sure?" I asked, still looking at Blaze.

"You know that our loyalty ain't never in question, but you wouldn't respect any of us if we didn't kick that real *shit* to you," Blaze said.

I knew that he was right, so I let it go and we rode the rest of the way in silence. When I brought the SUV to a stop at my house, no one immediately got out, like they were unsure of what needed to happen next.

"Blaze, grab that nigga and let's go. Kat, it's been fun," I said, grabbing my gun as I opened the door and hopped out.

Blaze went to the trunk to get *big hands*, Kat climbed back behind the wheel of the SUV, and Fabian followed me up the driveway. When I was walking past my Range Rover

I put my hand on the hood, and I was surprised to find that it was still warm.

"Skii should've got here hours ago, right?" I asked softly, stopping and turning to Fabian. "Yeah, probably sometime this morning. Why?"

I thought about that for a moment, tuning into my instincts because something was giving me a bad vibe. I looked toward the garage, and that was the first time I noticed that it was closed. We only closed the garage when the Range Rover was in there.

"Stay right here," I said, moving quietly toward the garage while keeping my eyes on the house.

When I got to the garage and saw the silver Aston Martin, I quickly moved back toward Fabian while checking to see how many bullets were left in my hundred-round drum.

"What's up?" Fabian asked.

"Somebody is in my house," I replied.

"You mean somebody besides Kyndra and Skii?" Blaze asked.

"Yeah," I replied, staring at my house like it was foreign territory and looking for signs of what could be happening behind closed doors.

Process of elimination told me that only one or two people could be here, because no one knew about this spot except for my brother and Tink. I damn sure hadn't invited either of them though.

"So what do you wanna do?" Fabian asked.

"Come on," I said, leading the way to the front door.

I used my thumbprint in the scanner attached to my Ring Cam to let us in, and as soon as the door opened all of my senses were on high alert. I could smell blood. I turned and pointed to my gun so that Fabian would know to pull his *shit* out because there was definitely hostility in the air.

"Honey, I'm home," I called out, doing my best to sound casual.

"I'm in the dining room," Kyndra replied.

I could hear the tightness in her voice, signaling that her stress levels were elevated. When I rounded the corner I quickly dissected what I was seeing— from the blood still leaking from Macy's head wound, to the fear on Skii's face. Kyndra was calmly seated at the head of the table beside Skii, Tink was standing behind both of them, and Jayson was posted up against the wall behind Macy, cradling my shotgun in his arms.

"What are you doing here?" I asked, tightening the grip on my pistol.

"Do I need a reason to come visit my brother and sister-in-law?" he countered.

"Based on the fact that one of my people is leaking, I'd say that you came for more than a casual visit," I replied.

I could feel Fabian behind me, but I hadn't moved far enough into the room for him or Blaze to be seen. I wanted to know what Jayson's intentions were before I acted on the hostility coursing through my veins.

"Me and Macy just had a slight misunderstanding, because for some reason she thought that I wasn't allowed in your house. That's funny, right?" he asked, not smiling in the slightest."It wasn't any type of misunderstanding. She was simply following orders and not letting *anyone* in my house," I replied.

"Oh… and I'm just anyone now?" he asked, letting the shotgun swing down until he was holding it pointed at the floor.

"You sounding real hurt, my nigga. You need a hug from your big bruh?" I asked, opening my arms wide.

"Maybe later. Right now I just came to the conclusion that we need to divide our assets, starting with the platinum and gold bars," he said.

"Last time I checked, that wasn't *our* heist. It was my wife and her crew who masterminded that. So how would you and I split that up?" I asked.

"Because I speak for Tink, and she wants her share," he replied.

My eyes shifted to Kyndra's cousin, and I could immediately sense how uncomfortable she was right now. She knew this wasn't gonna end well, and yet she had to remain loyal to the father of her unborn child. I understood her predicament, but I'd still blow her *thoughts* up against my dining room wall if shit popped off.

"Well, that's a conversation for another time, because right now I've got business to attend to. Put him on the table," I said over my shoulder as I stepped to the side.

Fabian came in first and posted up next to me while Blaze laid *big hands* out on the dining room table.

"Oh my God," Tink said, before she leaned over and became violently ill.

My eyes stayed on Jayson because I could see him calculating how all of this changed his odds and eliminated the advantage he thought he had. When he looked down at what used to be *big hands'* face, I could tell that he was shaken, but he was working hard to keep that fact hidden.

"Kyndra, you get to decide how this ends," I said, locking eyes with her.

There was no emotion anywhere on her face as she looked from her father to me and back to him, but I knew that there was at least some relief that it was over. She leaned over and whispered something to Skii, who then handed her a pistol. I could sense that Jayson was getting nervous, and undoubtedly it was because he knew he was outgunned.

"Daddy... daddy, can you hear me?" Kyndra asked, leaning closer to him.

big hands moaned in pain, but his eyes didn't open.

"It's okay, Dad. You're okay now," she said soothingly.

Hearing these words allowed him to open his eyes, and he looked straight up at his only daughter.

"Kyn... Kyndra, help me," he begged weakly.

"I will," she said, placing the pistol to the side of his head against his temple.

"Wait—"

Whatever plea he was gonna offer was lost in the thunderous boom of the gun in my wife's hand going off. His last thoughts sprayed the table right in front of Tink, causing her to lean over and vomit again.

"Did she eat chicken?" I asked, wrinkling my nose.

Jayson moved like he was going over to Tink, which was a mistake because he took his attention off of me long enough for me to raise my gun.

"Do me a favor, bruh, and put that shotty down on the table nice and slow. If you flinch, I'ma turn your world black," I vowed, leveling my pistol for a headshot that I wouldn't miss.

He hesitated, but it was brief because he knew I would do what I said, so he put the shotgun down.

"Macy, grab that for me," I instructed.

"Kwan, you need to remember that he's your brother," Blaze said.

"Oh, I know exactly who he is. Judas was somebody's brother too though, and we know how that turned out," I said.

"So what are you gonna do, Kwan… shoot me?" Jayson asked.

I thought about his question for a long moment.

And then I put my finger on the trigger.

Chapter 14

Kyndra

The emotions pumping through me were so overwhelming that I almost missed what was transpiring right in front of me, but I knew that look in Kwan's eyes. He was gonna kill his brother.

"Wait, just wait a minute," I said, taking a step back from my father's dead body.

Nobody else moved and no one spoke, but Kwan glanced at me long enough for me to know that he was listening to me for the moment.

"What are we doing? I mean, we're all family, so is this how we really wanna play this out?" I asked.

"Correction, *we were* family until Jayson and Tink left you alone at this nigga's mercy," Kwan said gesturing toward my late father.

"Tink is pregnant, and you wanted me to send her into a gunfight, my nigga. That didn't make sense," Jayson said.

"But it made sense for her to plot that crazy-ass scheme with Kyndra and go along? She wasn't too pregnant then, but as soon as *shit* hit the fan you both wanna hide behind the fact that she's pregnant. What about the fact that Kyndra's pregnant?" Kwan asked, sounding more agitated by the second.

"It's not that simple, and you know it," Jayson replied.

"Ain't it though," Kwan said, unwavering in his belief.

128

"You're awfully quiet, Tink. You don't have anything to say?" I asked, looking over at her."I–I just froze up. I didn't know what to do," she replied softly.

Part of me felt bad for her because I knew what it was like to fear for the life of an unborn child. At the same time I couldn't bring myself to lie to her and act like I'd forgiven her. I hadn't. I truthfully didn't know how to.

"Everybody needs to just take a deep breath because this *shit* is getting too heavy," Blaze said."He's right," Fabian agreed, pulling Kwan's arm down so that he wasn't pointing the gun at his brother anymore.

This didn't cause Jayson to relax any, but at least he was still breathing.

"There's a lot of history between all of us, and that can't be overlooked just because of one fuck-up," Blaze said.

"It can never go back to how it was," Kwan said with absolute certainty.

I wasn't about to argue because I knew he was right, even though it hurt somewhat because I'd literally grown up with Tink. We were like sisters, and I knew that Kwan and I were feeling the same sense of loss in that area.

"You're right, it can't go back to how it was, so just give us our cut of the gold and platinum, and we'll be on our way," Jayson said.

"Betrayal don't come with a severance package. Be thankful that you get to leave with your life," Kwan said in a low, threatening tone.

"Come on, Kwan, you two have always been partners. We *all* have," Blaze said, still trying to be the voice of reason.

"I don't give a fuck about none of that. I said he ain't getting *shit*," Kwan growled through clenched teeth.

I could visibly see his agitation getting ready to go next level, and that was the last thing that I wanted to happen.

"$100,000,000," I said impulsively.

"What?" Kwan asked, looking at me.

"I want you to give them a hundred million dollars and be done with it," I said.

"You know that what we stole is worth more than that," Tink said.

"Is it worth your life?" I asked, looking at her so she would see how serious this *shit* was.

"Take the money," Blaze said, looking at Jayson.

I'd thought that a number that big would defuse the situation, but it had only succeeded in taking the tension up a few notches.

"What about everything else?" Jayson asked.

"I assume you're talking about your share of the other jobs that you've pulled together. You'll get your cut, and nothing more," I said, leaving no room for negotiation.

"The same goes for you too, Tink," Kwan said.

"So we're just supposed to take the money you're offering, and tuck our tails between our legs?" Tink asked, letting her own frustrations show.

"You're lookin' at *shit* the wrong way, cuz. All you really need to focus on is you and your baby," I said, still trying to sound reasonable.

"Nah, Tink is right," Jayson said.

"You wanna be right, or you wanna live?" Kwan asked in a deadly serious tone.

"Kyndra can do a lot of things, but she can't kill me. So I'ma need more than what's being offered for all the work I've put in," Tink said.

Neither I nor Kwan responded, but I could feel what he was thinking and it mirrored my own feelings.

"Tink, I fuck wit' you, but right now you got me fucked up and confused with somebody else. Did you see what I just did?" I asked, gesturing toward my father with the gun that was still in my hand."I saw you, but shooting him ain't the same as shooting me and you know that," she replied confidently.

"Ayo, fuck all this back and forth. Get the fuck out my house," Kwan said angrily.

I was about to echo his sentiment because I was over the current conversation, but suddenly Jayson made a move to grab the shotgun from Macy and *shit* went bad quick. Kwan must've been watching him from the moment his body weight shifted, because as soon as his hand reached toward the shotgun, Kwan shot him in the very same hand. Jayson screamed out in pain as he clutched his left hand and fell back into the wall. I saw Tink jump out of the chair from my peripheral vision, and my gun was immediately on her.

"Think it through," I said, knowing that I'd shoot her if she made me.

"He needs help, dammit!" she said loudly.

"He needs to learn to follow basic instructions," I replied dispassionately.

The look she turned on me was so full of hatred that I could damn near *smell* the heat coming from her eyeballs.

"Blaze, if you want either of them to live beyond the next 30 seconds, I suggest that you get them out of here and out of Greece," Kwan said menacingly.

Blaze wasted no time going to Jayson and helping him off the wall while whispering to him that he needed to keep pressure on the wound. Tink moved slowly to follow them, and I didn't take my eyes off them until they'd disappeared down the hallway toward the front door.

"Kyndra, check Macy's head. Fabian, move that body out back, and Skii, you keep eyes on Jayson and Tink until they're on a plane headed out of the country. They're traveling in a silver Aston Martin," Kwan said.

We all moved without saying a word, but undoubtedly we were all thinking about what had just transpired here. There would be repercussions, but that wasn't something I could worry about right now. After grabbing a hand towel from the kitchen, I went to Macy and placed it gently against the side of her head.

"I'm okay," she said softly.

"I know, but your head is still bleeding."

She put her hand on top of mine and looked at me.

"You know that this ain't over, right?" she asked.

I wanted to lie to her and tell her that nothing would come of this falling out, but in my heart I really didn't believe those words. The odds that this would end well were slim and none, and right now Fabian was disposing of *slim* out back.

"I know it ain't over… just like I know we'll come out victorious in the end. There are no other options."

To be continued…

Lock Down Publications and Ca$h Presents
Assisted Publishing Packages

Due to an increase in the price of services we have increased our prices. The prices below reflect the price increase as of 11/1/24.

BASIC PACKAGE **$699** Editing Cover Design Formatting	UPGRADED PACKAGE **$1000** Typing Editing Cover Design Formatting Upload eBooks to Amazon Upload Paperback to Amazon
ADVANCE PACKAGE **$1,400** Typing Editing (line editing/content) Cover Design Formatting Copyright Registration Proofreading Upload eBooks to Amazon Upload Paperback to Amazon	LDP SUPREME PACKAGE **$1,700** Typing Editing (line editing/content) Cover Design Formatting Copyright Registration Proofreading Set up Amazon Account Upload eBooks to Amazon Upload Paperback to Amazon Advertise on LDP's Amazon and Facebook Page

***

Other services available upon request.
Additional charges may apply

Lock Down Publications
P.O. Box 944

Stockbridge, GA 30281-9998
Phone: 470 303-9761
Email: lockdownpublications@gmail.com

Submission Guideline

Submit the first three chapters of your completed manuscript to ldpsubmissions@gmail.com. In the subject line add **Your Book's Title**. The manuscript must be in a Word Doc file and sent as an attachment. Document should be in Times New Roman, double spaced, and in size 12 font. Also, provide your synopsis and full contact information. If sending multiple submissions, they must each be in a separate email.

Have a story but no way to send it electronically? You can still submit to LDP/Ca$h Presents. Send in the first three chapters, written or typed, of your completed manuscript to:

LDP: Submissions Dept
P.O. Box 944
Stockbridge, GA 30281-9998

DO NOT send original manuscript. Must be a duplicate.
Provide your synopsis and a cover letter containing your full contact information.

Thanks for considering LDP and Ca$h Presents.

NEW RELEASES

BLOODLINE OF A SAVAGE 1-3
THESE VICIOUS STREETS 1-3
RELENTLESS GOON 1-3
BY PRINCE A. TAUHID

THE BUTTERFLY MAFIA 1-3
BY FUMIYA PAYNE

A THUG'S STREET PRINCESS 1&2
BY MEESHA

CITY OF SMOKE 3
BY MOLOTTI

GET IT IN SLUGS 1 &2
BY B. STALL

STANDING ON HER BUSINESS 1&2
BY DG SANTANA

STEPPERS 1,2&3
THE REAL BADDIES OF CHI-RAQ
BY KING RIO

THE LANE 1&2
BY KEN-KEN SPENCE

THUG OF SPADES 1&2
LOVE IN THE TRENCHES 2
CORNER BOYS
BY COREY ROBINSON

TIL DEATH 3

KILLA CREW 2 | ARYANNA

BY ARYANNA

THE BIRTH OF A GANGSTER 4
BY DELMONT PLAYER

PRODUCT OF THE STREETS 1-3
BY DEMOND "MONEY" ANDERSON

NO TIME FOR ERROR
BY KEESE

MONEY HUNGRY DEMONS 1-2
BY TRANAY ADAMS

HUB CITY MENACE 1-3
BY J. WHITE

A THUGGISH PASSION 1&2
LAND OF DA HOOLIGANZ 1-4
KILLAZ ON STANDBY 1&2
BY IRA B.

FO'EVA ROLLIN 1&2
BY ASSA RAYMOND BAKER

THE LEVEL UP 1&3
BY LUXURY KING

Coming Soon from Lock Down Publications/Ca$h Presents

IF YOU CROSS ME ONCE 6
ANGEL V
By Anthony Fields

A THUGS STREET PRINCESS 3
By Meesha

CORNER BOYS 2
By Corey Robinson

THA TAKEOVER
By Keith Chandler

BETRAYAL OF A G 2
By Ray Vinci

SAVAGE FAMILY EMPIRE 1&2
SOULLESS GOON 1,2&3
THE DIRTY SIDE OF MONEY 1,2&3
By Prince

FOR MY ENEMY'S SAKE
AMBITIONS OF A SLIDER
FRESH OFF DA PORCH
By IRA B.

BY THE TRUCKLOAD 1-4
TIPPIN' THE SCALES 1-3
BAD BITCHES WIT GUNZ 3
PROBLEM SOLVED 2

By Christopher "Diesel" Hornezes

Available Now

RESTRAINING ORDER 1 & 2
By **CA$H & Coffee**

LOVE KNOWS NO BOUNDARIES 1-3
By **Coffee**

RAISED AS A GOON I, II, III & IV
BRED BY THE SLUMS I, II, III
BLAST FOR ME I & II
ROTTEN TO THE CORE I II III
A BRONX TALE I, II, III
DUFFLE BAG CARTEL I II III IV V VI
HEARTLESS GOON I II III IV V
A SAVAGE DOPEBOY I II
DRUG LORDS I II III
CUTTHROAT MAFIA I II
KING OF THE TRENCHES
By **Ghost**

LAY IT DOWN I & II
LAST OF A DYING BREED I II
BLOOD STAINS OF A SHOTTA I & II III
By **Jamaica**

LOYAL TO THE GAME I II III
LIFE OF SIN I, II III
By **TJ & Jelissa**

IF LOVING HIM IS WRONG…I & II
LOVE ME EVEN WHEN IT HURTS I II III
By **Jelissa**

PUSH IT TO THE LIMIT

KILLA CREW 2 | ARYANNA

By **Bre' Hayes**

BLOODY COMMAS I & II
SKI MASK CARTEL I, II & III
KING OF NEW YORK I II, III IV V
RISE TO POWER I II III
COKE KINGS I II III IV V
BORN HEARTLESS I II III IV
KING OF THE TRAP I II
By **T.J. Edwards**

WHEN THE STREETS CLAP BACK I & II III
THE HEART OF A SAVAGE I II III IV
MONEY MAFIA I II
LOYAL TO THE SOIL I II III
By **Jibril Williams**

A DISTINGUISHED THUG STOLE MY HEART I II & III
LOVE SHOULDN'T HURT I II III IV
RENEGADE BOYS 1-4
PAID IN KARMA 1-3
SAVAGE STORMS 1-3
AN UNFORESEEN LOVE 1-3
BABY, I'M WINTERTIME COLD 1-3
A THUG'S STREET PRINCESS 1&2
By **Meesha**

A GANGSTER'S CODE 1-3
A GANGSTER'S SYN 1-3
THE SAVAGE LIFE 1-3
CHAINED TO THE STREETS 1-3
BLOOD ON THE MONEY 1-3
A GANGSTA'S PAIN 1-3
BEAUTIFUL LIES AND UGLY TRUTHS
CHURCH IN THESE STREETS
By **J-Blunt**

CUM FOR ME 1-8

139

KILLA CREW 2 | ARYANNA

An LDP Erotica Collaboration

BLOOD OF A BOSS 1-5
SHADOWS OF THE GAME
TRAP BASTARD
By **Askari**

THE STREETS BLEED MURDER 1-3
THE HEART OF A GANGSTA 1-3
By **Jerry Jackson**

WHEN A GOOD GIRL GOES BAD
By **Adrienne**

THE COST OF LOYALTY 1-3
By **Kweli**

BRIDE OF A HUSTLA 1-3
THE FETTI GIRLS 1-3
CORRUPTED BY A GANGSTA 1-4
BLINDED BY HIS LOVE
THE PRICE YOU PAY FOR LOVE 1-3
DOPE GIRL MAGIC 1-3
By **Destiny Skai**

A KINGPIN'S AMBITION
A KINGPIN'S AMBITION II
I MURDER FOR THE DOUGH
By **Ambitious**

TRUE SAVAGE 1-7
DOPE BOY MAGIC 1-3
MIDNIGHT CARTEL 1-3
CITY OF KINGZ 1&2
NIGHTMARE ON SILENT AVE
THE PLUG OF LIL MEXICO 1&2
CLASSIC CITY
By **Chris Green**

A GANGSTER'S REVENGE 1-4
THE BOSS MAN'S DAUGHTERS 1-5
A SAVAGE LOVE 1&2
BAE BELONGS TO ME 1&2
A HUSTLER'S DECEIT 1-3
WHAT BAD BITCHES DO 1-3
SOUL OF A MONSTER 1-3
KILL ZONE
A DOPE BOY'S QUEEN 1-3
TIL DEATH 1-3
IMMA DIE BOUT MINE 1-6
DYING FOR LIKES
By **Aryanna**

A DOPEBOY'S PRAYER
By **Eddie "Wolf" Lee**

THE KING CARTEL 1-3
By **Frank Gresham**

THESE NIGGAS AIN'T LOYAL 1-3
By **Nikki Tee**

GANGSTA SHYT 1-3
By **CATO**

THE ULTIMATE BETRAYAL
By **Phoenix**

BOSS'N UP 1-3
By **Royal Nicole**

I LOVE YOU TO DEATH
By **Destiny J**

I RIDE FOR MY HITTA

I STILL RIDE FOR MY HITTA
By **Misty Holt**

LOVE & CHASIN' PAPER
By **Qay Crockett**

TO DIE IN VAIN
SINS OF A HUSTLA
By **ASAD**

BROOKLYN HUSTLAZ
By **Boogsy Morina**

BROOKLYN ON LOCK 1 & 2
By **Sonovia**

GANGSTA CITY
By **Teddy Duke**

A DRUG KING AND HIS DIAMOND 1-3
A DOPEMAN'S RICHES
HER MAN, MINE'S TOO 1&2
CASH MONEY HO'S
THE WIFEY I USED TO BE 1&2
PRETTY GIRLS DO NASTY THINGS
By **Nicole Goosby**

LIPSTICK KILLAH 1-3
CRIME OF PASSION 1-3
FRIEND OR FOE 1-3
By **Mimi**

TRAPHOUSE KING 1-3
KINGPIN KILLAZ 1-3
STREET KINGS 1&2
PAID IN BLOOD 1&2
CARTEL KILLAZ 1-3
DOPE GODS 1&2
By **Hood Rich**

THE STREETS ARE CALLING
By **Duquie Wilson**

STEADY MOBBN' 1-3
THE STREETS STAINED MY SOUL 1-3
By **Marcellus Allen**

WHO SHOT YA 1-3
SON OF A DOPE FIEND 1-4
HEAVEN GOT A GHETTO 1&2
SKI MASK MONEY 1&2
By **Renta**

GORILLAZ IN THE BAY 1-4
TEARS OF A GANGSTA 1/&2
3X KRAZY 1&2
STRAIGHT BEAST MODE 1&2
By **DE'KARI**

TRIGGADALE 1-3
MURDA WAS THE CASE 1-3
By **Elijah R. Freeman**

SLAUGHTER GANG 1-3
RUTHLESS HEART 1-3
By **Willie Slaughter**

GOD BLESS THE TRAPPERS 1-3
THESE SCANDALOUS STREETS 1-3
FEAR MY GANGSTA 1-5
THESE STREETS DON'T LOVE NOBODY 1-2
BURY ME A G 1-5
A GANGSTA'S EMPIRE 1-4
THE DOPEMAN'S BODYGAURD 1&2
THE REALEST KILLAZ 1-3
THE LAST OF THE OGS 1-3
By **Tranay Adams**

KILLA CREW 2 | ARYANNA

MARRIED TO A BOSS 1-3
By **Destiny Skai & Chris Green**

KINGZ OF THE GAME 1-7
CRIME BOSS 1-4
By **Playa Ray**

FUK SHYT
By **Blakk Diamond**

DON'T F#CK WITH MY HEART 1&2
By **Linnea**

ADDICTED TO THE DRAMA 1-3
IN THE ARM OF HIS BOSS
By **Jamila**

LOYALTY AIN'T PROMISED 1&2
By **Keith Williams**

YAYO 1-4
A SHOOTER'S AMBITION 1&2
BRED IN THE GAME
By **S. Allen**

TRAP GOD 1-3
RICH $AVAGE 1-3
MONEY IN THE GRAVE 1-3
CARTEL MONEY 1&2
By **Martell Troublesome Bolden**

FOREVER GANGSTA 1&2
GLOCKS ON SATIN SHEETS 1&2
By **Adrian Dulan**

TOE TAGZ 1-4
LEVELS TO THIS SHYT 1&2
IT'S JUST ME AND YOU

KILLA CREW 2 | ARYANNA

By **Ah'Million**

KINGPIN DREAMS 1-3
RAN OFF ON DA PLUG
By **Paper Boi Rari**

THE STREETS MADE ME 1-3
By **Larry D. Wright**

CONFESSIONS OF A GANGSTA 1-4
CONFESSIONS OF A JACKBOY 1-3
CONFESSIONS OF A HITMAN
CONFESSIONS OF A DOPE BOY
By **Nicholas Lock**

I'M NOTHING WITHOUT HIS LOVE
SINS OF A THUG
TO THE THUG I LOVED BEFORE
A GANGSTA SAVED XMAS
IN A HUSTLER I TRUST
By **Monet Dragun**

QUIET MONEY 1-3
THUG LIFE 1-3
EXTENDED CLIP 1&2
A GANGSTA'S PARADISE
By **Trai'Quan**

CAUGHT UP IN THE LIFE 1-3
THE STREETS NEVER LET GO 1-3
By **Robert Baptiste**

NEW TO THE GAME 1-3
MONEY, MURDER & MEMORIES 1-3
By **Malik D. Rice**

CREAM 2-3
THE STREETS WILL TALK

KILLA CREW 2 | ARYANNA

By **Yolanda Moore**

THE STREETS WILL NEVER CLOSE 1-3
By **K'ajji**

LIFE OF A SAVAGE 1-4
A GANGSTA'S QUR'AN 1-4
MURDA SEASON 1-3
GANGLAND CARTEL 1-3
CHI'RAQ GANGSTAS 1-4
KILLERS ON ELM STREET 1-3
JACK BOYZ N DA BRONX 1-3
A DOPEBOY'S DREAM 1-3
JACK BOYS VS DOPE BOYS 1-3
COKE GIRLZ
COKE BOYS
SOSA GANG 1&2
BRONX SAVAGES
BODYMORE KINGPINS
BLOOD OF A GOON
By **Romell Tukes**

CONCRETE KILLA 1-3
VICIOUS LOYALTY 1-3
BLOODY MONEY BAGS
By **Kingpen**

THE ULTIMATE SACRIFICE 1-6
KHADIFI
IF YOU CROSS ME ONCE 1-3
ANGEL 1-4
IN THE BLINK OF AN EYE
By **Anthony Fields**

THE LIFE OF A HOOD STAR
By **Ca$h & Rashia Wilson**

NIGHTMARES OF A HUSTLA 1-3

KILLA CREW 2 | ARYANNA

BLOOD AND GAMES 1&2
By **King Dream**

GHOST MOB
By **Stilloan Robinson**

HARD AND RUTHLESS 1&2
MOB TOWN 251
THE BILLIONAIRE BENTLEYS 1-3
REAL G'S MOVE IN SILENCE
By **Von Diesel**

MOB TIES 1-7
SOUL OF A HUSTLER, HEART OF A KILLER 1-3
GORILLAZ IN THE TRENCHES
OOPS CRY TOO 1&2
THE DAUGHTER OF A CARTEL BOSS
By **SayNoMore**

BODYMORE MURDERLAND 1-3
THE BIRTH OF A GANGSTER 1-4
By **Delmont Player**

FOR THE LOVE OF A BOSS 1&2
By **C. D. Blue**

KILLA KOUNTY 1-5
TENDER
By **Khufu**

MOBBED UP 1-4
THE BRICK MAN 1-5
THE COCAINE PRINCESS 1-10
STEPPERS 1-3
SUPER GREMLIN 1-4
A GANGSTA'S SON
By **King Rio**

MONEY GAME 1&2

KILLA CREW 2 | ARYANNA

By **Smoove Dolla**

A GANGSTA'S KARMA 1-5
By **FLAME**

KING OF THE TRENCHES 1-3
By **GHOST & TRANAY ADAMS**

BAD BITCHES WIT GUNZ 1&2
PROBLEM SOLVED
By "Christopher Diesel" Hornezes

QUEEN OF THE ZOO 1&2
By **Black Migo**

GRIMEY WAYS 1-3
BETRAYAL OF A G
By **Ray Vinci**

XMAS WITH AN ATL SHOOTER
By **Ca$h & Destiny Skai**

KING KILLA 1&2
By **Vincent "Vitto" Holloway**

BETRAYAL OF A THUG 1&2
By **Fre$h**

COUNTDOWN OF A KILLA 1&2
SEX, MURDER AND GOD 1&2
GUNS DOWN, BOTTOMS UP 1&2
By Lo-Life

THE MURDER QUEENS 1-7
By **Michael Gallon**

FOR THE LOVE OF BLOOD 1-4
By **Jamel Mitchell**

HOOD CONSIGLIERE 1&2
NO TIME FOR ERROR
By **Keese**

PROTÉGÉ OF A LEGEND 1,2&3
LOVE IN THE TRENCHES 1&2
By **Corey Robinson**

THE PLUG'S RUTHLESS DAUGHTER 1&2
By **Tony Daniels**

BORN IN THE GRAVE 1-3
CRIME PAYS
By **Self Made Tay**

MOAN IN MY MOUTH
By **XTASY**

TORN BETWEEN A GANGSTER AND A GENTLEMAN
By **J-BLUNT & Miss Kim**

LOYALTY IS EVERYTHING 1-3
CITY OF SMOKE 1-3
By **Molotti**

HERE TODAY GONE TOMORROW 1&2
By **Fly Rock**

WOMEN LIE MEN LIE 1-4
FIFTY SHADES OF SNOW 1-3
STACK BEFORE YOU SPLURGE
GIRLS FALL LIKE DOMINOES
NAÏVE TO THE STREETS
By **ROY MILLIGAN**

PILLOW PRINCESS

KILLA CREW 2 | ARYANNA

By **S. Hawkins**

THE BUTTERFLY MAFIA 1-3
SALUTE MY SAVAGERY 1&2
By **Fumiya Payne**

THE LANE 1&2
By Ken-Ken Spence

THE PUSSY TRAP 1-5
By **Nene Capri**

DIRTY DNA
By **Blaque**

SANCTIFIED AND HORNY
by **XTASY**

BOOKS BY LDP'S CEO, CA$H

TRUST IN NO MAN
TRUST IN NO MAN 2
TRUST IN NO MAN 3
BONDED BY BLOOD
SHORTY GOT A THUG
THUGS CRY
THUGS CRY 2
THUGS CRY 3
TRUST NO BITCH
TRUST NO BITCH 2
TRUST NO BITCH 3
TIL MY CASKET DROPS
RESTRAINING ORDER
RESTRAINING ORDER 2
IN LOVE WITH A CONVICT
LIFE OF A HOOD STAR
XMAS WITH AN ATL SHOOTER

www.ingramcontent.com/pod-product-compliance
Lightning Source LLC
Chambersburg PA
CBHW071228260626
47162CB00004B/1461